Fractured Desires

Book Three

Fallen

Jezza Deep

Dedication

To my Paramore, even apart we are always together.

Table of Contents

Prolouge

Past

The knock on the door sounded innocent enough light and almost pleasant. But it wasn't.

The man at the battered old desk knew that. His dirty bruised head jerked up from the lines of coke he was snorting through a cut straw, his face blanching whiter than the powder scattered across the scarred tabletop. Whiter than the filthy t-shirt he wore, which was torn and stained with old sweat.

He suspected death was standing outside his door. Not realizing that a far more dangerous foe was already inside, watching from the tattered couch, cloaked in invisibility.

Malik narrowed his eyes, observing as the man leaped from his chair, his pupils so dilated they nearly eclipsed the blue of his irises. Blue, as her eyes will be, he thought, fidgeting with impatience. He wanted to get this over with, but not yet. Better to let the man's fear boil over, let desperation claw at him until he'd do anything, pay any price, to save his life.

The man Andras was in trouble with people who didn't knock twice. They'd shoot him in the face and leave his body to rot, unnoticed, in this seedy dive. The kind of place where hollow-eyed tenants pretended you didn't exist if you did the same for them. It didn't matter to Malik what happened to this waste of life except that Andras had something he needed and a man on the brink of death would part with anything for the promise of deliverance.

The knock came again, louder this time. Andras's trembling hands rummaged through a desk drawer, pulling out a pistol. Flattening himself against the cracked drywall, he crept toward the door, his breathing ragged and desperate. The room, dimly lit by a single shaft of grimy sunlight, felt stifling as his heart pounded dangerously fast fueled by coke and panic. Malik imagined it would give out before the bullets did.

The idiot opened his mouth to call out.

Now.

Malik dropped the shield that kept him invisible to human eyes and replaced it with one that cloaked them from the world outside, wrapping them in a bubble of silence and stillness. The clock on the wall stopped ticking. Traffic noises from outside ceased.

Blinking in confusion, Andras scanned the room until his gaze landed on Malik, lounging on the couch. His eyes widened in horror, and the pistol jerked upward, aimed at his chest.

Malik grinned lazily. "You're going to die."

"Fuck you," Andras rasped, pulling the trigger.

One…two…three… shots rang out, punching four neat holes in the back of the couch. Malik yawned, showing his boredom as the man emptied the clip into the furniture. Andras kept pulling the trigger until only empty clicks echoed in the silence.

"Are you quite finished?" Malik asked, his tone dripping with disdain.

"How the… who the hell…?" he stammered, breathing wild and erratic. The gun slipped from his fingers and clattered to the floor.

"I'm not who you think I am, obviously," Malik said with a cold smile. "Or I'd be bleeding out on your hideous carpet right now. But here's the thing, Andras, you'll get a close look at that carpet soon enough. In about two minutes, the man outside will blow so many holes in you, that I'll be able to see daylight through your body."

Malik stood, stretching as if unconcerned by the man who was moments away from death. Andras slid down the wall, his eyes wide, fists clenching and unclenching as he muttered.

The sight of Andras's pathetic terror almost disgusted Malik enough to end it right there. But it wasn't his soul he was after. This miserable wretch would end up in Hell soon enough. Hell was patient when it came to trash like him. But Malik's goal was far more precious.

"Get up," He ordered, voice hard. Andras stared blankly at him, his mind too scattered to respond.

With a swift kick, Malik knocked his head back against the wall, cutting off the string of incoherent prayers from the man's lips. "I said, get up."

Without waiting he grabbed him by the collar and hauled him to his feet, dragging him to a nearby chair. Andras collapsed into it, shaking, his bloodshot eyes fixed on Malik in terror.

"What do you want from me?" he croaked, wiping at the blood trickling from his split lip.

Malik steepled his fingers and leaned in, locking his burning red gaze on the man. "I want to save you."

Andras blinked, confusion momentarily overtaking his fear. "You've got a hell of a way of showing it."

"I don't sugarcoat things you're in deep shit, and for a price, I'll get you out of it... this time."

"What—?"

"I don't like repeating myself." Malik's voice was icy. "I can save you from what's coming, but it won't be free."

Andras glanced at the door, panic gnawing at him. "What do you want? Money? Drugs?"

Malik's expression darkened, and he leaned forward, his voice low and dangerous. "Your daughter."

Andras froze, disbelief flickering across his face. "I ain't got no daughter."

"You do, her name is Aurora and she's seven months old."

Malik leaned in until they were nearly nose to nose, watching as realization slowly dawned on Andras's face. "I want her," Malik said, his voice soft but deadly.

The man's mouth opened and closed, trying to process what he was asking his mind, sluggish and drug-addled, stumbled over memories of a forgotten club night.

"What does it matter to you?" Malik pressed. "You forced yourself on her in the bathroom just another mistake in a long line of sins. The girl's nothing to you. But to me, she's everything."

Andras stared, unable to find the words.

"You have two choices," he continued, feigning indifference. "Let them kill you or give me the girl. She'll never know you existed either way."

"I'll do it," Andras blurted his voice shaking. "Take her. I don't care…get me out of here."

Malik felt a wave of triumph surge through him. After centuries of searching, of waiting she was finally his. He stood, pulling a scroll from his coat... the contract.

"Sign this," he said, spreading the parchment on the coffee table. "Her soul for your life... simple."

Andras's eyes scanned the document, his jaw tense. "How do I sign?"

Malik produced a quill, slashing the man's hand with a quick swipe of his fingernail. As blood welled up, Andras took the quill and signed over his daughter's soul without hesitation.

Malik's grin widened as he rolled up the contract, the weight of centuries lifting from his shoulders. She was his now.

"Get out of here," Malik said, his voice devoid of the earlier malice. "Before someone decides to finish what they started."

He nodded, trembling as he stumbled to the door, his breaths ragged with relief. "Thank you."

Malik turned his back on him, tucking the contract inside his coat. "Save your thanks," he muttered as he stepped into the night. "I'm sure we'll be seeing you again soon enough."

Chapter 1

"Shit, shit, shit." Aurora staggered on her heels, hurrying down the sidewalk. She was late. Again. How it kept happening, she had no idea. James was not going to be pissed. She could already hear his reprimand echoing in her head, sharp and cold.

Rounding the corner, the restaurant came into view, separated from her by a steady stream of city traffic. She focused on the red *Do Not Walk* light and frantically jabbed the button.

"Come on, come on!" Her newly reset watch read 7:51 over twenty minutes late. Oh, forget "not thrilled" he would be livid. She'd tried calling him, but he hadn't picked up. Whether he'd silenced his phone or was ignoring her, she didn't know.

He cared about appearances, about what others thought except, it seemed when it came to her. Their entire relationship was balanced on a knife's edge, teetering toward disaster. One nudge could send it all crashing down, but maybe she was being paranoid. God knew it wouldn't be the first time.

Tonight, she'd hoped to fix things, to finally talk about how miserable he'd been making her feel lately. Maybe, just maybe, they could work it out. The fantasy was that they'd end up at his place, laughing over old movies, making love all night like they used to when things were good.

But that dream was dead now.

The light changed, and she all but sprinted across the street—well, as much as she could in heels. Her arches screamed in protest by the time she reached the restaurant steps, she was breathless. She could hardly get the words out to the host about meeting someone already there. What if he had left? Oh God, the humiliation but she couldn't blame him.

Relief swept through her as the host led her toward the back, to their usual table he was still here, at least. Fuming, no doubt, but if his mood weren't too bad maybe they could still salvage the night. He hated tardiness and never failed to remind her that she was the most disorganized person he'd ever met.

It wasn't for lack of trying. Something... or someone seemed determined to keep her life in chaos. Like a cosmic prankster, always ensuring she was a mess, always keeping her off balance. And it was all building toward…something. She didn't know what, but it was bad all her life, she'd lived with a sense that the axe was ready to fall. It was only a question of when and how many necks it would sever.

James's brown hair came into view, and Aurora steeled herself. She slid into the chair the host pulled out for her, words of apology already forming on her lips. But when she met his eyes, simmering with barely contained anger those words died.

Her fingers twisted nervously in her lap. She tried again. "James, I'm—"

"What was it this time?" he interrupted. "Flat tire? Wardrobe malfunction? Alien abduction?"

All my clocks were wrong every one of them.

The excuse sounded crazy, even to her. She'd thought she was on time until she saw the clock in her car and then the sign at the bank. Then there was the DJ on the radio confirming the truth. Giving up on an explanation that would make sense, she sighed. "I'm sorry. That's all I can say."

"It wouldn't be such a big deal if it didn't happen *all* the time," he snapped.

"I get that you're upset, and I deserve it. But can't we talk about this another—"

"I don't get you," he said, as if she hadn't spoken. "You're getting worse."

"Worse?" The word stung more than it should have.

"You're never on time your absentminded, clumsy, and the nightmares? They're getting more intense. You're *seeing* things, Aurora. I think it's time you saw someone a professional."

Her heart thudded painfully in her chest. She could barely swallow past the lump in her throat. "You think I need a shrink? You think I'm crazy?"

"I didn't say that. Don't put words in my mouth."

"Then what *are* you saying?" Her voice wavered, but she pressed on. Deep down, she couldn't argue with him. The nightmares, the strange visions had been escalating. Things she'd seen since she was a child. She'd always ignored them, tried to push them away. But James saying it aloud made her blood run cold.

"The truth is, Aurora, you're scaring the hell out of me."

Her fingers trembled as she picked up her napkin, trying to smooth it over her lap. "Nothing is wrong with me," she lied. "I've just been preoccupied, all the other…weird stuff? That's stopped. It's been months." She avoided his eyes, taking a quick sip of water. "You're overreacting."

James's jaw clenched, his voice lowering into a near-hiss. "I'm not overreacting and it's not just about you being late all the time. Last weekend when you stayed over—"

She cut him off, her voice brittle. "What happened? Did I talk in my sleep again?"

"More than that." He paused, running a hand through his hair. "You screamed. You were talking about someone coming for you. When I tried to calm you down, you went catatonic."

She sucked in a breath, her mind reeling. "I don't remember any of that."

He hadn't mentioned it before. They'd spoken since only to arrange this dinner, but now she saw the distance in his voice, his silence. He'd been pulling away, and she hadn't even noticed.

His gaze softened, but his voice remained firm. "I'm telling you this because I care. You need help, Aur. You know I'm right."

The words hung heavily in the air between them. There was something else in his eyes, though something beyond concern.

"Oh my God," she whispered, her stomach dropping. "You're leaving me."

He sighed, the tension in his shoulders visible as he sat back. "This wasn't an easy decision."

"So, this is your parting advice?" Her voice cracked. "Get your head checked and have a nice life?"

"It's not like that—"

"Don't do that!" she snapped, louder than she intended. Several heads turned, and he cringed at the attention.

"I didn't want to do this here," he said, keeping his voice low. "But you and I both know we were headed for this... eventually."

"I hope that makes you feel better," she said bitterly, her laugh sharp and humorless. "But that was a shitty thing to say, just for the record."

A muscle twitched in his jaw; he was close to losing his temper. "I didn't *want* to do this tonight."

"Oh, just picking the perfect moment to drop the axe, huh?" She stood abruptly, her pulse hammering in her ears. The panic, the denial, and the horror tangled into a knot of emotion too big to contain. Snatching her purse from the floor, she slung it over her shoulder.

He rose and stepped in front of her his hand on her arm. "Don't leave like this. We can still—"

"Let go of me." Her voice was cold, sharp as glass. "Before I show you *psycho* right here in front of everyone."

He released her, hands up in surrender. The hurt in his eyes nearly undid her. It wasn't fair that at that moment, he looked sexier than ever. Once, she'd dreamed of marrying him, of building a life together, perfection at long last.

But she was never meant for perfection.

"Goodbye, James," she whispered, walking past him.

He didn't follow.

Chapter 2

From the shadows, Malik watched her. Aurora burst through the restaurant's front doors, stopping at the iron railing. One hand grasped the cold metal, and the other flew to her mouth, stifling a sob. For a moment, she hesitated, her gaze flicking back toward the door, before she bolted down the steps, putting as much distance between herself and the restaurant as possible. Thunder rumbled overhead.

This could be it if he wanted it to be. Her fate had always been in his hands, it had been since the day she was born. One subtle manipulation of the stoplights, and she could easily be struck by an oncoming car. A clean, quick death or he could approach her now, face-to-face, and with a single touch, rip her soul from her body he hadn't decided yet.

Either way, it would end centuries of wanting. She'd be his, at last for eternity.

She was so vibrant. Some souls shined so brightly they were given more than one turn on earth, capable of doing immeasurable good. Souls so pure his kind didn't even dare corrupt them. She was one of those old souls timeless, radiant.

But this cycle was different. Somehow, she'd been dealt a bad hand, and Malik had found a weak spot where he could worm his way in. He didn't care how or why. He only cared that he'd been patient and patience always paid off.

A gust of wind from the approaching storm swept down the street as he silently moved beside her at the corner. She stared blankly ahead, waiting for the light to change, tears streaming down her cheeks. A delicate profile, like something from an old worn photo timeless, tragic. Her shiver was so slight that no one else noticed, but he did. Her body knew he was there, even if her mind didn't.

Someone asked her if she was okay. She waved them off with a dismissive nod focusing still on the street ahead. The light changed, and she stepped off the curb.

No. Not this way.

He wasn't ready, the moment wasn't right. He didn't understand why, but she fascinated him. Her soul was ripe for the taking, but still, he lingered watching, waiting. There would be a better moment, he could feel it. She wasn't quite ready, and neither was he.

"So, here we are again. When do you plan to take her?"

The voice cut through the downpour like a blade, crystal clear despite the sudden sheets of rain. Malik stiffened, cursing under his breath. He was invisible to human eyes, which could only mean one thing…

He turned slowly to find a figure standing behind him, glowing with that insufferable, blinding golden light, tunic, tainia headband... the whole bit. Malik smirked; the theatrics never ceased to amuse him. "I was wondering when you'd show up."

Sol's gaze followed Aurora as she crossed the street, sadness etched in his ethereal face. They were all the same to him, arrogant, self-righteous... useless.

Malik turned his back on him, dismissing him with a flick of his wrist. "You're wasting your time I've waited eons for this. Nothing is going to stop me now. Save your breath she's mine."

"She doesn't deserve this," Sol said softly, ignoring Malik's provocation. "At least give her more time."

"For what? So, you can try to sabotage me?" Malik scoffed. "Your interference only makes me want to act faster. Perhaps tonight, as she sleeps, I'll rip her soul out and take her home. I'll show her what she's been missing all these centuries."

"She doesn't deserve this," he repeated, his voice laced with sorrow. "I suppose telling you how disgusting you are—"

"Makes no fucking difference," Malik growled, his patience slipping. He started across the street, following Aurora's hurried steps. "Fly away, little butterfly."

Sol didn't budge. "This won't be the last you see of me, demon."

Malik paused mid-step, glancing back with narrow eyes. "You'll be too late."

"I doubt that."

But when Malik turned to snarl a retort, the god was gone, typical... nimble bastards.

No matter Aurora was rounding the corner toward the parking garage. He could still take her now, prove that godly prick wrong.

He followed her, the sound of her heels clicking sharply against the pavement drawing him closer. Her scent lingered delicate sweet pea mixing with the fresh rain. Her red hair clung damply to her shoulders; black dress hugged her every curve. She was breathtaking, even now, soaked, and distraught. His mind flickered to an image of his hands gripping her ankles, pulling them apart, sliding over her skin while she writhed and begged beneath him…

There was a sharp crack, and suddenly she pitched to the right with a startled gasp. Her arm flailed out, reaching for something, anything to break the fall.

Instinctively, Malik moved.

Later, he would curse himself for it. But at that moment, without thinking, he dropped his shields and caught her just before her head hit the curb. Her body was warm and trembling in his arms, her breath catching in her throat as she stared up at him in shock.

Thunder boomed overhead.

Her eyes, wide and crystalline, locked onto his. They were the same as they had been for centuries, crystal, blue, and full of life. Her lips parted in a soft gasp, her tears mingling with the rain on her cheeks.

Shit.

That fucking prick God had been right.

Chapter 3

"Oh my ...," She gasped as the stranger lifted her to her feet. Her legs wobbled beneath her as she regained her balance. "I'm so sorry. My… the heel broke." She bent over, inspecting the snapped heel with a trembling sigh. "Perfect ending to a shitty night."

"Sorry to hear that," he replied, though the ironic edge in his voice didn't sound sorry at all.

"It's no big deal. I hardly wear them anyway," she said placing a hand on her chest, trying to slow her racing heart. If he hadn't caught her…

"Are you all, right?"

She nodded, then gave him a better look. Black hair, tan skin. He was dressed simply in black jeans and a dark shirt. But how had he caught her so quickly? He must have been right on her heels. The thought sent a shiver of cold dread through her. She hadn't even heard him approach, and no one else was around…

He stood there watching her, his gaze steady and unsettling, as if studying her for something she didn't understand. Her breath hitched as she realized she was still trembling.

Suddenly, she became aware of how much of a hit mess she looked wet hair, streaked makeup, and her dress sticking to her skin. She glanced down, mortified. One foot bare, the other still in her broken shoe. She was tempted to cross her arms over her chest but resisted. It wasn't like she was showing much cleavage. Still, under the dress, her body reacted traitorously nipples tightening beneath the slinky fabric, her skin tingling under his gaze.

"Where did you come from?" she asked when it became clear he wasn't going to say anything. Trying to distract herself from the intensity of his eyes, she pulled off her other shoe and stood barefoot. Her feet sighed in relief.

"I was right behind you, heading to my car. Almost tripped over you." He shrugged, broad shoulders shifting under his shirt. "You should buy better shoes you could have killed me." His smirk was sharp, and teasing, and suddenly she noticed how striking he was. His mouth was perfectly shaped, his eyes dark and deep, like they held secrets.

"A guy encouraging me to buy better shoes? I might've hit the lottery," she blurted, cringing at how flirty it sounded.

The smirk broke into a smile that crinkled his eyes. Despite herself, she smiled back, even though her instincts told her to keep her guard up. He was handsome, yes but there was something wicked behind that smile, a dangerous edge she couldn't quite place.

"Well," she said, feeling a rush of awkwardness again. "Thank you for, uh… saving me. I've got to get going."

"Aside from the death of a shoe, what's made your night so bad?" he asked, his voice threaded with curiosity.

She hesitated. His attention felt good, especially after James's brutal rejection, and the way he looked at her like she was the only person that mattered right now made her pulse quicken.

A car sped by, making her jump. He was waiting for an answer.

"Oh, I don't want to dump all my problems on you," she said, trying to deflect.

"What a shame," he said with a slow grin. "I'm a really good listener."

There it was again that low, seductive tone. His voice was deep, rich, and carried a subtle accent she couldn't place. It curled through her, making her want to hear more of it. To have it whispered in her ear while his hands—

Stop.

Her heart was pounding for a different reason now, her mind betraying her. She barely knew this man, but the thought of inviting him home flickered like a dangerous temptation. It would be easy too easy, to let the night take her somewhere reckless. James had left her humiliated and now this dark, mysterious stranger had caught her, made her feel something. But she wasn't that girl... was she?

Her relationships had always been disasters one after another. Even with James, she'd thought things were different, thought she'd finally found stability. She'd forced herself to take it slowly, to play by the rules but even that had blown up in her face.

Nothing ever worked.

Frustration burned bright in her chest as she stared at the man in front of her. If nothing she did worked, then why not try something else? Something she'd never dared before just this once.

"Aurora?"

The voice stopped her cold. James. Of course.

Her shoulders sagged as she turned, biting back a groan. "What?"

He stood a few paces away, his gaze moving over her in that infuriatingly familiar way taking in the broken shoe, the ruined makeup, the wet hair. "Are you all, right?"

There it was again. *Are you all, right?* How many times had he asked her that? When she woke up screaming, when strange things happened when her life unraveled bit by bit. He had asked, but never really listened.

"You know what, James? No, I'm not all right. You're big on me not denying my problems, right? Well, there you go. I'm not all right. Does that make you feel better?"

His face tightened, and his voice dripped with anger. "To hell with you."

She winced, the words hitting harder than she expected. But when she glanced at the stranger, he didn't seem fazed by the squabble, if anything, his attention remained fixed on her. Calm, watchful. Maybe she'd misread him entirely because he wanted nothing to do with this disaster of a situation.

"Please leave," she said quietly.

James scowled at her, then shot an odd look at the stranger before walking away without another word. For a moment, she thought James was going to say something, maybe warn the guy off but he didn't, he simply left.

Aurora turned back to the stranger, heat rising to her cheeks. "Well, you just witnessed one of the low points of my existence, and I don't even know your name."

He smiled, but it didn't quite reach his eyes. "Call me Malik."

Malik the name hit her like a bolt of electricity. Something about it felt… dangerous. But in a way she couldn't resist, could she really go through with this? Could she ask him to come with her?

"I'm Aurora," she said, forcing a smile to cover her nervousness. "I guess you could call me Aur, after tonight."

He chuckled softly. "Well, Aurora, I hope your night improves."

It could. *You could help,* she thought, her heart racing again. But his tone sounded like a farewell, of course it did. Why would someone like him stick around for this train wreck? Her disappointment gnawed at her, but she swallowed it down.

"Thanks again for helping me. Good night."

He gave a slight nod. As she walked away, she felt the tension in her body slowly released. The moment she was out of his sight, she realized how strange she had felt around him like something was off, but she couldn't place it. Now that she was alone, the hair on the back of her neck settled her lungs expanded with relief as if she'd been holding her breath the entire time.

Her white mini came into view, and she climbed inside, laying her head back against the seat. Tears squeezed from between her closed eyelids.

James was right, something was wrong with her. She was unraveling, and it was becoming impossible to ignore. Maybe she did need help. Maybe she needed—

No.

She sat up straight, a wave of frustration surging through her. No padded rooms. No more doubts. There was something *real* behind the nightmares, the visions, the strange things she couldn't explain, and whatever it was, she had to find it. To understand it.

She turned the key in the ignition, but nothing happened. Silence.

"You've got to be fucking kidding me."

Chapter 4

He was out of his fucking damned mind, which was the only explanation for why she still drew breath. At any moment, he could have reaped what was his, and yet something in her pleading blue eyes had stopped him cold. He'd sensed it when he touched her, the torment swirling inside her misery she wore like a second skin. Of course, much of it was his own doing, side effects of his claim on her soul. But when he glimpsed the pain, her lover had just caused, a flash of something dark and primal had surfaced, a desire to rip the man's soul out.

He was disappointed the human wasn't corrupt enough to warrant such a delicious fate.

Instead, his focus had remained on her, his fascination growing. Her emotions, clear and raw, played out on her face anger, frustration, sorrow. He could feel them even without touching her and for all the havoc he'd wrought on her soul, he wasn't reveling in his triumph. He had broken her down, stripped her of the strength and purity they sent her back to earth with. But instead of relishing the victory, he found himself hesitating.

She was desperate, weak, and afraid. He should have been laughing, savoring the moment. He'd managed to taint one of the God's most cherished. This could be his rise back to greatness, a victory that would elevate him back into Lucifer's ranks.

All he had to do was take her.

But he couldn't. Not yet.

From the shadows of the parking structure, he watched her climb into the car. The hem of her dress slid up her thigh, baring her skin down to her delicate, bare foot. His mouth watered. His cock stirred an ache building that he hadn't felt in centuries. He reached out with his power and disabled her car's engine. It wasn't time for her to leave yet.

He wanted to probe deeper, to touch her again, feel her softness beneath his fingertips. He'd grown used to the hard desolation of his world. But a few more touches of her silken skin, and he might grow attached to this one.

He moved toward her car, watching as she rested her head on the steering wheel, her shoulders trembling with quiet sobs. Her hair spilled down her back like a curtain of dark silk, catching the faint glow of the overhead lights. She looked so small and fragile.

Maybe she'd tell him to leave, maybe she'd be afraid of him.

But Malik raised his hand and tapped on the window anyway.

Her head jerked up, eyes widening as they met his through the glass. She quickly wiped at her cheeks and popped the door open. "Um, hi," she said, her voice raw from crying. Despite her effort to compose herself, her face was still damp.

"Are you having trouble?" he asked.

She laughed, but there was no humor. It was one of the most despairing sounds he'd ever heard. "If you only knew what a loaded question that is."

Oh, he did know. "I can help, Aurora."

She softened at the sound of her name. Her eyes fluttered closed for a moment before she shook her head. "No, you can't. No one can. It's not just the car... it's every God damn thing."

"He doesn't deserve you," he said, knowing he was no better.

She sucked in a breath, her gaze snapping back to his, lips parting in surprise. "You don't know anything about me. How can you say that?"

He reached out, gently grasping her chin between his fingers. "I don't have to know you, I have eyes." His gaze trailed down her body, lingering where the bodice of her dress clung to her breasts. She was lush and curvaceous... beautiful. His thumb stroked her cheek, and her eyes fluttered closed and she leaning into his touch.

He could have her for eternity, but he wanted her now, while she was still vibrant, alive. He wanted to taste the salt of her tears, to breathe in the spicy heat of her arousal.

Her lips trembled. "Do I know you? Have we met before?"

Interesting. She couldn't have seen him, but perhaps she sensed him near her, recognized the energy between them. He smiled, a touch of reassurance in the curve of his lips. "Maybe in another life."

"This is so not me," she whispered.

"What's that?"

"I don't know you."

"I thought we just established that you do, somehow."

A small smile tugged at the corner of her mouth. "You know what I mean."

He leaned in, lowering his voice to a hushed murmur. "You don't know me, and yet… you want to. You wonder if it's wrong to let go, just once in your life.

His finger slid down her neck, pausing over the frantic beat of her pulse. She tensed but didn't pull away. He could feel her confusion, her desire. What would it feel like to bury himself inside her, to feel those emotions crest as she came apart in his arms?

"And it's all right," he whispered, his finger tracing the edge of her neckline. "There's no one to impress anymore, no one to judge you."

"What if I judge myself?" she asked softly.

"Guilt is useless."

She let out a shaky breath. "I think you might be a bad influence."

He smiled, his fingertip just grazing the fabric of her dress. "Let me be. Take me home with you."

She hesitated before glancing toward the front of her car. "I hope your ride is nearby."

He grinned, leaning into the car. Reaching across the steering column, he turned the key. The engine roared to life, and Aurora gasped, eyes wide with disbelief.

"What the…? A minute ago, it was dead! How did you do that?"

He straightened, shrugging with mock innocence. "I guess I have the magic touch."

Her heart was racing from the way his finger had burned a path across her skin, her body thrummed with need. As they drove to her apartment the silence between them was thick with tension. She glanced at him watching the streetlights cast fleeting shadows over his face. Every time she looked away, she told herself he wasn't that good-looking, only to be proven wrong when she looked again.

By the time they pulled into the parking lot of her building, her nerves were on fire. "Here we are," she said, her voice tight.

Everything about tonight felt wrong and surreal. She knew herself when she'd left her apartment, but now… she wasn't sure who she was anymore.

"What's wrong?" he asked. "Second thoughts?"

She swallowed hard. Her mind screamed that this was the wrong choice, that she was crossing a line she couldn't come back from.

But then he reached over, placing a hand on her back and all the swirling doubts and fear dissipated. His fingers slid down her spine, each touch soothing the storm inside her.

"My boyfriend broke up with me tonight," she blurted.

"I figured as much."

"Right before I met you. Now here I am, with you, and…" She trailed off.

"This isn't you," he finished.

"It's not," she whispered.

"Why do you think you have to convince me?"

"Well…" Her words faltered as his fingers traced a slow, sensual path back up her spine. Her entire body was electrified under his touch. Her skin burned with need, with an ache that pulsed through her veins. "Do you want to know why he left me?"

He shrugged, his voice a low rumble. "Does it matter?"

He leaned in closer, his breath warm against her ear. "You're so worried about what I'll see, what terrible secret are you hiding."

The massaging fingers became firm, biting into the tender flesh. She couldn't fight his grip when he turned her head to face him, and she didn't want to. His mouth was so close to hers that his breath stole hers between her lips.

The way he spoke of dark, terrible secrets made all of her anxieties seem like child play. That was how she felt with him suddenly, like a child compared to someone much older and infinitely knowledgeable.

"I don't have any dark secrets," she muttered, her breath shaky.

His gaze darkened, lips curling into a knowing smile. "Of course you do."

"No, I—"

"Tell me why he left you."

"He thinks I'm crazy." Rolled off her tongue as if it didn't even shame her, though it did. Now he would probably release her like she had the plague and never look back. When he didn't, she was compelled only to keep talking, pushing him, daring him. "He thinks I need a psychiatrist. I see things. Like…these dead souls in mirrors that reach for me. I dream about stuff I can't even describe to you, stuff that makes me wake up screaming and fighting the empty air and I don't know why I'm telling you this—"

"Don't stop."

She found she couldn't. "He thinks I'm too clingy. Oh, I need a shrink. I'm the weak one what he doesn't realize is if he saw half the crazy shit I did, he would be in a padded fucking cell by now."

He grinned a slow, wicked smile that sent a thrill of heat through her body. He was still touching her, still looking at her like she was the most fascinating woman he'd ever seen.

"See?" His voice dropped even lower, his lips brushing her ear. "That wasn't so bad, was it?"

"I've made it this far, so I'm doing fine. I'm upset at him, but I don't need someone to…to rescue me."

His lips brushed the outer ridge of her ear. "Mumm. Was it a hero you were looking for?"

She sucked in a breath, especially when his lips parted and trailed lower, to her neck. Her pussy ached so bad she squeezed her thighs together, trying to assuage the building demand. "I…might have been. Whether I wanted to admit it or not."

His hand dropped to her leg, the entire appendage jumped at the touch, and her hand flew down to grasp his. The sudden movement only assisted his hand in slipping under her dress, his hot fingers curling around her rigid muscle. "Maybe tonight I can fill that role," he murmured.

All she knew was that she wanted him to fill something.

"Maybe tonight, Aurora, we can do what we can to save each other." Any remaining resistance inside her broke. She turned her face to his and sought his mouth with hers, finding it even hotter than the rest of him and just the perfect balance between soft and hard. His gentleness surprised her and sent her desire spiraling. Her hand abandoned his and she curled her arms around his neck, drawing him closer and leaving him free to explore her body as he wished. She wanted those hands all over everywhere, right now. His tongue slid between her lips and their mutual groans mingled together, his gruff hers breathless.

He tasted like pure heat and sin, and before she realized it, she was tilting her hips toward him, silently inviting his hand to slip farther up her thigh. She spread her legs wider, she was wet, burning up, excruciatingly aware of the emptiness throbbing in her pussy. "Please touch me," she begged against his lips, but he was cruelly content taking his precious time.

He did touch her, but not where she needed him most. His hand moved up to her left breast, cupping its weight as his thumb circled her tightly budded nipple through her dress and bra. God, she needed these clothes off, she needed his clothes off. As if he'd read her mind, he abandoned his exploration to grasp the strap of her dress and yank it off her shoulder. He shoved the cup of her strapless down and, despite her earlier plea, apprehension overtook lust, and she cast a glance out the windshield.

"We should go inside," she said.

His reply was to lean down and kiss the bare swell of her breast. She couldn't help it; she arched into him, stroking his silky soft hair. His tongue swirled around her nipple and then his lips fastened to it, sucking her so deep and hard it stung. She cried out, the throb in her pussy so intense she bucked against the empty air in a vain attempt to ease it.

He obviously had no intention of quenching that need for her not in the way she expected. He had her other breast bare now and he divided the attentions of his mouth between them, licking and sucking one, fondling the other, until they were as heavy and aching as her pussy.

Her entire body felt enraptured with need, and all she could think about was him plunging into her molten core. How good it would be. Good was too weak, but damned if her brain could be bothered to think yet conjure up another. It would be so good, the mere thought of those delectable thrusts was enough to drive her over the edge. For the first time in her life, she shuddered with climax while nothing at all touched between her legs.

When she came to herself, she was sprawled backward, half lying against the door while he leaned over to reach her. She vaguely remembered crying out words but couldn't remember for the life of her what she'd said. Her hair was in her face, her skin tingled all over in the aftermath, and Malik looked down at her with dark eyes. They reflected nothing, not even the overhead lamps outside.

She stared at him in amazement. "No one's ever done that to me before. I mean, made me cum…like that."

"Pity."

She agreed… wow. If he could do that barely touching her, what could he accomplish if he had rein of her body? As he withdrew to his seat and she set about fixing her clothes, she hoped he was about to show her.

Chapter 5

Malik had indulged in pleasures of the flesh many times over the years, but none had tasted as sweet as Aurora. Whether it was because she'd been his forbidden fruit for so long or because there was something different about her—something more enticing than any other woman he'd encountered—he couldn't be sure nor did he care.

She unlocked her door, leading him inside, her fingers trembling slightly as she flipped on a light. It was dim, but not enough to hide the blush still burning in her cheeks from their interlude in the car. He longed to put his lips to that flushed skin again, to taste her until dawn, to unwrap her body and revel in her softness all night.

She wandered toward the kitchen, pushing her hair back with her hand. "Would you like something? A drink, or...?"

He smiled, but the only thing he craved was her. "No," he said softly, then, remembering the importance of mortal courtesy, he added, "Thank you."

"Okay." She exhaled slowly, her nerves clear as she met his gaze briefly, biting her lip before turning away. "I'm going to have a glass of wine."

He could already imagine the flavor of the wine lingering on her lips, mixing with her natural sweetness. While she busied herself in the kitchen, he let his gaze roam over the space. It was familiar, but tonight different charged with anticipating what was to come. It was small but tidy, flashes of her personality shining through the imperfections: colorful pillows decorating the worn couch, unique vases on the tables, and books lots of them, they lined the shelves, small stacks on the coffee table. He could picture her curled up with reading glasses perched on her nose as she escaped into one of those worlds.

He had watched her do them before mundane activities had always fascinated him, especially when it was her. She moved through life with a quiet strength, ignorant of the shadow looming over her. It made her bravery even more compelling. Most under contract would succumb to their fear, lives reduced to terror but not her. She soldiered on, completely unaware of her fate.

It almost disgusted him the pathetic man who had given her away so easily and, in some way, he was disgusted with himself as well.

She returned, wine in hand, and gave him a tentative smile. "Do you mind if I ask what you do?"

He waved dismissively. "Contracts it's boring work I'd hate to ruin the evening by discussing it. What about you?"

"I'm a waitress, and I help out at a friend's bookstore," she said, her lips brushing the rim of the wineglass.

He watched the liquid slide toward her mouth, imagining her lips elsewhere, and he smiled as her gaze briefly flicked toward him.

"How did you get the night off?" he asked, his voice teasing.

"It's rare," she laughed, "but I'm free tomorrow, too. I can't remember the last time I had a weekend off." Her gaze dropped again, but he didn't want to wait anymore. In a few strides, he reached her, taking the glass from her hand and setting it aside.

"Feel better?" he murmured, tracing a silky lock of hair with his fingertip.

"I do," she whispered, her voice soft. "Better than I have in a while."

His hands moved to her shoulders, slipping the straps of her dress down. It fluttered to the floor. She started to cover herself out of reflex but hesitated. He smiled at the gesture endearing, though unnecessary. The black lace of her lingerie barely covered her. His thoughts clouded with hunger as he drank in the sight of her, her breaths coming deep and steady, though he knew it must be a struggle to maintain that composure.

"Has anyone ever told you how exquisite you are?" he asked, his voice thick with desire.

She blinked, surprised. "Exquisite? No."

"And has anyone ever shown you?"

The question affected her for a moment he believed the glimmer in her eye was a welling tear, but her voice held no sign of its presence. "Not really, but that's okay."

It wasn't, these pathetic men in her life could have had her in ways he never could, and not one of them had ever treated her as the treasure she was. They could spend a lifetime with her, form an unbreakable bond based on trust and honesty, and love her every night of their lives until death took them. He could have her only by deception and underhandedness. He could only have her by stealing her.

Not one of those others had ever made her feel as she did now with only his gaze caressing her flesh. He knew because her emotions were coming through loud and clear. If he'd had a heart, it would be breaking for her. It was all his fault, he was the one who'd broken her she'd never really had a chance.

As if chains that had been holding her captive suddenly snapped, she surged forward grabbing his face between her hands, catching his lips with hers. Blind lust ripped through him, blazed a trail of heat through the tundra of his soul, and he met her on the same plane of hunger and desperation. Her soft body pressed tight to his, and her sweet pea scent swirled in his mind. Her warmth pervaded him.

Gripping her ass, lifting her against him, and headed instinctively to her bedroom, every step torture as she ground against the hardness of his cock his hard-on hadn't abated since the parking garage and now it bordered on painful. He almost missed the door and barely avoided slamming her into the frame. She giggled as he cleared it, her mouth unwilling to leave his. A little squeal escaped her as he tumbled them both onto the bed.

He paused staring down at her, smoothing the hair from her forehead. Her face was cast half in shadow and half in the light filtering in from the window. Split in two, light and dark, much like her soul. As he watched, her swollen lips parted, and the tip of her tongue swept the bottom. Ah, she was trying to kill him. He was nestled in the cradle of her thighs, and every tiny movement of her hips sent lightning through him. It might only be his imagination, but he could swear he felt the damp heat of her even through his jeans.

"This isn't fair," she whispered, her hands creeping under his shirt. "I'm damn near naked and you're not."

"It's a problem," he agreed, lifting so that he knelt between her thighs. Never taking his gaze from hers, he began taking off his shirt. She watched the progress of his hands, the pulse jumping at the base of her throat he could practically hear it drumming in his ears. He got his shirt up and almost over his head then she sat up and pressed her soft lips to his stomach, just above the edge of his jeans.

His muscles jumped at the contact, tensing when her wet little tongue connected with his flesh. A growl caught in his throat as he flung the shirt the rest of the way off; his hands sank into her hair hard enough to hurt, but she didn't utter a single sound. Instead, her fingers attacked the button of his jeans, and he grasped the opportunity to reach behind her and unhook the cursed bra that kept her hidden from his sight. She tore it away and yanked his jeans down his thighs, freeing his cock.

Bliss engulfed him, it was her hands on him wrapping around his cock, her warm breath tickling across the head. But if she laid those wet lips on him at this point, he would lose his last fragile grip on control.

He grasped the sides of her head, wrenching it upward crashing his lips into hers every bit was wild, their tongues dueling and teeth nipping. He propelled her backward again, catching his weight on his elbows.

"Malik, touch me," she whispered, surging her hips to rub against his erection. One barrier existed between them now, and it was torture he knew for damn sure how wet she was; the panel of her lacy black panties drenched, and he deliberately stroked the head of his cock over it as she arched against him. "Please. I can't wait any longer."

Oh, she had no idea about waiting, about agony. He wasn't too keen on teaching her about them, either. He'd had enough of both.

She gasped into his mouth as her panties snapped with one wrenching pull. The scent of her desire swirled in his head, intoxicating him. Her hands roamed his back, her nails gingerly scoring his flesh. She lifted her hips, causing his shaft to graze her wet clit, and the sound she made in his ear was nearly his undoing. Teeth clamped onto his earlobe, driving a curse from his lips.

He reached between them and slipped his fingers between her legs. Her legs fell farther apart, giving him more room to explore the damp, delicate tissues, the tight little bud he'd later like to spend an hour licking and sucking until she screamed or begged him to stop. With a tilt of her hips, his fingertip slid lower, seeking and finding the tight entrance to her body. Her hands clenched on his shoulders as the muscles of her inner walls fluttered around his finger, holding him, pulling him in, demanding more.

He wanted to whisper to her how long he'd wanted her, but it would prove catastrophic, she wouldn't understand likely, and she never would. This was his one opportunity to have her, and he wouldn't have given it up for all the souls in the world.

He squeezed another finger inside her and stroked, thrusting slowly in and out, building her need as her little cries lilted into the silence. Her hips found his rhythm and met it, rolling with it, her pussy so wet, so soft…

Then she moaned as he latched on to her nipple, sucking it into his mouth and holding it there mercilessly. He released her breast with an audible little pop. But he couldn't go far away; her hand was holding the back of his head, fisting in his hair.

He abandoned her breasts to move down her body, absorbing her shivers as he settled his shoulders between her thighs. Only then did he allow his finger to slide down, down, and slowly circle her clit.

Her moisture glistened in the scant light from the window and enticed him to taste it. Even in the darkness, he could see she was flushed and swollen with her need. She was as soft against his fingers as she looked, and he took his time touching her until his mouth watered for a taste. He slid two fingers into her drenched heat, listening to her breathing go out of control. Just the way he'd wanted. She stretched around the intrusion, so sweet, so accepting. Her own hands came down and found the backs of her knees, pulling her legs farther apart.

"Beautiful," he murmured, drawing his fingers out to their tips before slowly plunging in again over and over.

"Oh God," she cried. "Oh, yes. Don't stop."

To show her just how intent he was on not stopping, he leaned forward and closed his lips around her bud and felt her entire body shudder. Her taste exploded in his mouth, tangy and sweet, and he licked to lap up every precious drop of her arousal. He curled his fingers inside her bringing her ass off the bed, and caught her there with his free hand, holding her thrusting hips captive. Her hands released her knees and sank into his hair.

He felt it begin, the gripping heat of her pussy rippling around his fingers as the muscles in her thighs pulled tight as bowstrings over his shoulders. So much energy poured off her, so much emotion, and he soaked it up, drank her in, and craved more. More of her, her body and soul stripped bare and his for the taking. He held her to his mouth, nibbled and licked and suckled her through it until she collapsed, panting and cursing and trembling on the bed.

He crawled up the length of her, glad for the moment her eyes were closed and her face turned away because he had no idea what might be revealed in his expression. There had never been a more beautiful, vulnerable sight. It called to his inner beast and taunted it tempting it to run wild. One of her hands was on her forehead and the other fluttered to her chest as she tried to catch her breath, her breasts quivering. The silk of her inner thighs brushed his hips.

He slid his fingers under hers and felt the pounding of her heart beneath her breastbone. So strong and full of life. A life that was his for the taking. This was how it would begin, his dark energy would gather, and pulse through him into her. It would detach her spirit. It would hurt, and he wished he could avoid that, but it wouldn't last long, and then she would be his.... for eternity.

Chapter 6

She'd never had a problem reaching an orgasm but that one had been something else. Maybe there was something to this love-them-and-leave-them thing. It sounded cliché, but she was still seeing stars. Behind her closed eyelids, they twinkled and burst; for now, she was content to watch them. Anything to avoid looking at his face and risking falling headfirst into love, the very thing she didn't want. That's always where she got it wrong.

His fingers rested on her chest, right over her heart, slowly caressing. The weight of his hand made her feel strange, as though something inside her was pulling toward him, answering a silent call. A tingling, spreading ache crept through her limbs, making her shift uncomfortably. She wasn't in the mood for any weirdness not when she was floating so high on post-orgasmic bliss. *Malik,* she needed more of him, and she wasn't finished yet.

She clasped his hand, his skin so warm it nearly burned and guided it to her mouth. The strange ache vanished instantly as she kissed one of his fingertips, teasing it with her tongue before pulling it between her lips. When he groaned, she finally opened her eyes to look at him.

His face was tense brow furrowed as if in pain, not pleasure. His eyes were closed, his sensual lips parted, and his whole body seemed coiled with unspent energy.

Oddly enough, she felt a wave of gratitude wash over her. Tonight was supposed to be one of those miserable nights spent drowning in chocolate and alcohol, wallowing. If not for him, that's exactly where she'd be.

She'd still have to face tomorrow alone, but at least she'd shared this night with someone who made her laugh and made her feel good. The hard length of him pressed against her belly was a reminder she had unfinished business.

His eyes opened and locked onto hers, stealing her breath—not from any sappy notion, but from the raw, untamed promise she saw there. It wasn't love she saw in those depths; it was passion, wild and consuming the kind that would change her. The intensity in his gaze almost scared her, it also tempted her, reminding her of that moment in the car when she'd sensed a storm brewing. That storm was here now, ready to unleash its fury on her.

Words crowded her throat. She didn't know which to say first. *Fuck me, take me, make me not care if tomorrow comes...*

But all she managed was his name—and it was enough.

He fell on her like a man starved, his hand slipping behind her head, pulling her into a kiss that made her whole body ignite. She opened for him, parting lips and legs to let him closer, deeper. His tongue invaded her mouth as she craved for his body to invade the pulsing heat between her thighs.

Her pulse quickened as she took him in fully. He was long, thick, and already leaking with the promise of pleasure she could barely wait to taste.

He kissed her hard and she was lost again through a maelstrom of lust. His head found her entrance, feeling ten times bigger than it had looked, and the death she was anticipating, oh yeah, it was coming for her after all. She nearly came just from the touch of him there, and when he pushed…

The world ended and began again. He stretched her beyond the point of pain, but so many sensations mingled it was impossible to extract it from the pleasure. Her nails dug into his shoulders, she caught his hips in a death grip with her thighs.

"So, fucking good," he murmured in her ear. Good, she didn't think anything had ever felt so good. He was burning lava above her, inside her, damn, she melted around him. But he wasn't moving fast enough, he wasn't moving at all, and she needed to move.

"Please," she whispered, making a little circle with her hips, the most she could do with him pinning her to the mattress. "Malik, please."

A gruff sound came from his throat. Slowly, so slowly he pulled out inch by inch. Her body clung to him, gripped him, and protested his retreat. He withdrew until he was poised at her entrance again, slick with her juices.

His gaze drew back and found hers and his hips surged. The rhythm he set punished her. So wet now, so easy, she took him all, tossing her head on the pillow as ecstasy devoured her. He knew how to move, how to twist his hips to hit all her sweet spots, and she bit her lips on cries that would have her neighbors calling 911 because the quiet girl next door was being brutally murdered.

"Aurora," he groaned, every bit of pleasure he was feeling evident in his voice. He somehow flared even hotter against her. She was liberally slicked with sweat when he didn't seem to have broken one at all, and hers was as much from the heat he was generating above as the heat he was generating within. She didn't know if she could take much more without combusting.

"So close, I'm so close," she whispered hotly in his ear, as much to encourage him to keep doing it just like that as to hurry him along to his completion. She wanted to cum with him. It had never been something she cared about before and it was something that had rarely, if ever, happened. But everything about this had been so perfect she couldn't imagine a better ending than for both of them to fall into bliss together.

She felt the shudder and the tightening of her muscles began. She couldn't stave it off. It grew inside her, eclipsing her, frightening her with its power. A few more strokes, a few more brushes against her clit, and she'd be there, she'd be…

The building pressure crested and dissolved into rolling waves of mind-numbing pleasure. That storm she'd been waiting for, that fury blew over her, and she hung on to him as an anchor in all this wildness. She felt his hips jerk away from the smooth, sure rhythm he'd maintained, heard his rough groan in her ear, and knew that she'd gotten her wish. She wasn't alone in the storm.

It felt like the night stretched endlessly before them, and she was perfectly fine with that. He was the most insatiable lover she'd ever had. When they finally collapsed, utterly spent at least *she* was she half-expected him to get up, announce he was calling a cab, and leave.

But instead, they lay face-to-face, talking about nothing and everything, while his fingers traced lazy patterns on her arm.

Was this supposed to be part of the deal? She'd heard Renee's stories about her hookups, but none involved spilling your soul to a guy you'd likely never see again. Yet here was Malik, asking her questions, genuinely interested in her answers, though he offered little about himself in return. Eventually, she couldn't hold back her curiosity any longer.

"Why all the interest in me?" she asked, her voice quieter than intended.

He lifted his gaze, his eyes narrowing slightly. "What's that?"

"Why me? I know I fell into your arms tonight, but... what made you stick with me? I mean, I was a pathetic, weepy mess with obvious baggage." Her lips twisted with self-deprecating bitterness as another thought hit her, one that should've occurred earlier. "Was it pity?"

"No," he said sharply, without hesitation. "Never that. I'm not that kind of guy."

"Then what? I mean… I'm not usually this down on myself, but I can't imagine I looked that interesting. I'm hardly a 'sex siren' or anything."

A grin tugged at his lips, lips she realized she could stare at forever. "How lucky for us that I thought otherwise even luckier that I was right."

She gasped, feigning outrage. "Oh, really?"

They laughed, and the sound was warm and easy, as it faded, she couldn't shake the urge to press further. "Is it lame? Questioning your judgment like this?"

"Very lame."

"I told you, I'm not very good at this."

"You didn't say you wouldn't be good at it. You only said this wasn't you." He paused, his eyes roaming over her. "But I found you *very* good."

"Gee, thanks."

He didn't respond right away, just looked at her with that gaze that unsettled her. It was like he knew her, on some deep, unspoken level. She couldn't shake the feeling. Her phone buzzed on the nightstand, shattering the moment.

She'd forgotten to turn it off earlier, but she knew who it was. James had been calling and texting all night, and Malik had kept her too occupied to care. When she'd gotten up for a bathroom break earlier, she'd seen the display light up with his name. Malik watched her closely, reading the frustration, guilt, and sadness that must have shown on her face.

"Your boyfriend?" he asked quietly.

"Ex," she corrected.

"He doesn't seem happy about the 'ex' part."

"He should've thought of that before he made it official."

"And you? Are you okay with it?"

"No one likes getting dumped," she said, tracing her fingers over his shoulder. "But it does make things easier when someone's around to help pick up the pieces."

He watched her. "Do you love him?"

"I, um..." She hesitated, caught off guard. Did she? She was upset, sure, and it hurt like hell. But was she truly heartbroken? Or was she mourning something else, a sense of security, a future she thought she was building, the idea of normalcy and family?

He was still waiting for her answer, his gaze pressing into her. She didn't owe him a response, but the way he looked at her made her want to give one. "I cared about him, maybe even loved him. Or maybe love could have come eventually. I don't know."

"Did he ever make you feel like I did tonight?"

She frowned, surprised he'd ask something like that, especially in that smug, self-assured tone. Most guys didn't want to hear about their predecessors. But then, he was different.

She hesitated. For a fleeting moment, a chilling thought surfaced. What if he wasn't just some stranger passing through her life? What if he was dangerous? A psycho? The tattoos she hadn't noticed until he'd gotten up to get her a drink earlier. Elaborate black patterns, swirl across his back and down to his butt. The amount of detail, the pain it must have taken... What did they mean?

She'd asked, but he just shrugged and said they looked cool. Then he came back to bed and made her forget all about it for a while.

"I don't feel like discussing my sex life with James, if that's okay with you."

He scoffed. "Well, that answers my question. Aurora, he meant nothing to you. Those tears you shed for him? A waste."

She stared at him, then sat up, hugging herself as a sudden chill crept over her. "You say that like you know it for a fact."

"I do."

"You can't possibly."

"Everyone leaves you, don't they?"

Her breath caught. "What?"

"You push people away because you know they'll be gone eventually. That's why you let me in tonight. You expect me to be gone by morning. No surprises. No pain. Right? No family cause none of them are in your life anymore, are they? You're alone."

Who the hell *was* he, messing with her mind like this? "What does it matter to you? You *will* be gone tomorrow, so stop trying to psychoanalyze me. I already had that fight tonight. What are you some psych student? Am I just an experiment?"

He leaned in, skimming his hands up her bare arms, sending a shiver through her. His touch was electric, goosebumps rippling across her skin as his hand came to rest over her heart. It leaped toward him as if it wanted to feel the pressure of his fingers around it. A small, helpless sound escaped her throat. *What the hell is wrong with me?*

"I'm sorry," he whispered, his lips brushing her shoulder. He kissed a slow trail up to her neck, and against her better judgment, she tilted her head to give him access. Even after everything, she melted under his touch. "But you intrigue me. So much."

Why? She'd asked him that already, but he wouldn't answer. She wished he would... wished he could say something that made sense of all this, something that would make the pieces of her life fit together.

But that was ridiculous. Wasn't it?

Still, the thought wouldn't leave her alone.

"Everyone leaves me," she whispered, surprised when the words escaped her lips. Once they were out, she couldn't hold the rest back. "You're right. But I've learned to deal with it. I've learned to build walls and not let anyone get too close."

It had all started with her mother. Sad that she could trace the unraveling of her life so precisely *if* it had ever been together in the first place. A child could only endure so many lies before distrust took root. She remembered standing at the funeral, looking at the thin, waxy figure in the casket, and feeling nothing. That body had never truly loved her, never been a mother.

And now, she realized she *wanted* to let it all out. Maybe she needed therapy or just *this*. Someone to hold her, to not question her pain or her sanity. Someone to whisper that it would be okay, even if it was just for tonight.

"I'm sorry, Aurora. That you were hurt," he murmured, his lips brushing her ear. His voice held a softness she hadn't expected, as if he *meant* it. The tenderness caught her off guard, making her wonder if anything he'd said tonight had been real.

"I'll be fine, always have been," she replied, her voice shaking, hoping he'd hear it and make the tremble disappear.

Chapter 7

The nightmare returned. It was never the same, but the darkness within them was constant, an oppressive shadow lurking beneath every scene like a foul signature. She knew these dreams well as soon as they started, but that knowledge never gave her any control. She was trapped, helpless, until the dream was done with her, leaving her teetering at the edge of madness. The force was there each time, a relentless wind pushing her toward the precipice, daring her to fall into the void.

She woke screaming, thrashing her way out from the twisted, damp sheets, her body fighting against the skeletal hands that clawed at her, skeletal fingers trying to pull her down. They were burying her alive, trapping her in the earth where black, fetid dirt filled her mouth and nose. She could feel it choking her, robbing her of air until she couldn't—

Firm hands caught her, stronger than the ones from her nightmare. She flailed wildly, hitting at them, but they held her fast, wrapping around her wrists and pinning her down with an undeniable force.

"Aurora. You need to wake up." The voice cut through the terror, low and steady, carrying a command that reached deep inside her.

Her eyes snapped open. Her hair stuck to her damp face, blurring her vision, but she blinked and slowly her surroundings became focused on her room. The dim, early light creeps in through the window and Malik. He was still here, still with her.

His grip on her wrists eased, but his expression stayed tense, his eyes searching hers for some sign she had fully returned.

Before she could think, she blurted out, "I'm sorry!" The words slipped out, a reflex, something she'd said a hundred times to James when she'd woken him up like this.

He let go of her completely and lay back beside her and without hesitation, he drew her into his arms, pulling her against him. She rested her cheek against his chest, inhaling his warmth, wishing she could dissolve into him. She wasn't crying, she never cried—but her body trembled uncontrollably. The steady rise and fall of his chest were the only thing keeping her from unraveling.

"It's okay," he whispered into her hair, his voice a balm to her frayed nerves. For a moment, she believed him.

The minutes slipped by, and the panic began to fade. But in its place, shame rose, thick and heavy. She kept her face hidden, pressing into his skin, not wanting to face him. She didn't owe him an explanation—he'd be gone by morning... she was sure. That was the pattern. Better to stay quiet, let it go, and let him slip away.

Reality beckoned. It would be a relief, but the nightmare lingered at the edges of her thoughts, unwilling to fully let go. She tried to focus on her breathing, forcing herself to inhale and exhale slowly, but her body wasn't ready to cooperate.

Then, without warning, he tilted her face up and kissed her it was unexpected. She didn't even have time to worry about the usual morning trivialities... she was lost.

He tasted like comfort his lips moved softly against hers, coaxing them open, his tongue teasing her in a way that made her toes curl. The sensation was slow, and deliberately it banished every last trace of the nightmare.

How did he do this? How did he always manage to drive away the darkness?

"Better?" he murmured, barely pulling back, his lips grazing hers in lazy, playful kisses.

She gave a soft hum of agreement, surprised by the sound of her voice. She sounded calm, even content.

He laid her head back against his chest, his fingers gently stroking her hair. "Try to sleep again."

The suggestion was tempting but it came with a small pang of fear. "I don't know if I can. The dreams—"

"I'll be here. I'll keep them away."

His words were foolish, maybe even a little too romantic, but they worked.

...

As usual, Renee was running late to her store. Aurora didn't mind; she unlocked the door and disarmed the security system, it was nearing eleven.

At least she'd managed a few more hours of sleep after Malik had left. The goodbye had been strange, awkward even. He wanted to say something but hesitated, eyes flickering with indecision before he finally kissed her goodbye.

The truth was, she knew next to nothing about him. No phone number, no last name, no address. That ball was firmly in his court now and if she was honest with herself, she hoped he'd play it. So much for her "love them and leave them" approach.

Renee bounced in thirty minutes later, Dunkin in hand and carrying a donut box, looking like she'd just rolled out of bed. Her usually sleek blonde hair was flat and lifeless today, and she was hiding behind a pair of oversized sunglasses.

Aurora glanced at the box, raising an eyebrow. "I was just thinking about lunch."

"I'll eat all this and whatever you get for lunch. I'm starving." Renee tossed the box onto the counter and dove into a donut-like she hadn't eaten in days a blissful expression crossed her face with the first bite.

Aurora reached over, tugging the sunglasses off her face, tilting her chin to inspect her eyes. "No hangover? Impressive."

She grinned around her mouthful of donuts. "Nope. Didn't even go out last night."

"Really? I tried calling you."

"I crashed early."

"What's going on with you?"

She shrugged, finally sipping her coffee after demolishing half the donut. "You got me a Boston cream, right?" Aurora asked, reaching for the box.

"It's lunchtime," Renee teased, pushing the box toward her. "But of course I did."

"How did your date go last night?" She'd been waiting to ask. Aurora had confided in her about her hopes for the evening.

She took a deep breath. "You won't believe it. Seriously. If this were April Fool's, you'd accuse me of trying to pull something on you."

Renee's eyes widened, her curiosity piqued. "What happened? Did he propose?"

"He dumped me."

Her mouth fell open. "What?! That bastard! But… wait, hold on—what?" She blinked at Aurora, taking in her appearance. "You don't look like you got dumped. You're… glowing? I mean, seriously, you look like you're about to flash a new diamond ring or something."

"It makes sense once you hear everything."

"What, did you break up and then have make-up sex? Is that it?"

"No, no. There's no making up with James. But… there *was* sex."

Renee's expression froze mid-bite. The look on her face was priceless, and Aurora couldn't hold back her laughter. "You should see your face right now," she giggled.

"With who?" she demanded, eyes wide.

"Oh, Ren I met a guy by accident and ran into him in the parking garage after dinner. He was incredible. Gorgeous, sexy, and we barely talked, but… well, I brought him home."

"Holy Shit!" She was momentarily stunned. "Speechless. You've rendered me speechless this *never* happens."

"I know, right?"

"So… details! Spill!"

Aurora shook her head, a wistful smile spreading across her face. "Let's just say he was amazing, and I don't regret a second of it." She sipped her coffee, watching Renee's reaction.

She leaned back, shaking her head in disbelief. "Damn. I feel like a proud mom like my little Aurora is all grown up now."

"Let's not be ridiculous. It was just… one of those things. It got my mind off everything and, you know, it reminded me there's more out there, James isn't the only man out there."

"So, are you going to see this guy again? At least tell me his name!"

Aurora hesitated. "Malik… but that's all I've got I doubt I'll see him again. It was just… a moment."

"Aurora to *me* it would be just a moment. But to you? Are you sure you're okay with this?"

Memories of the night before flooded back his hands, his eyes, the way his body moved against hers. She could still feel the ache where he'd touched her. She waved her hand, pretending to focus on the stack of books by the register. "I'm fine."

"You like him."

"Well, yeah. But so, what? I'm a grown woman I made the decision, and I can handle it."

"So, what's James's problem, then?"

"He… doesn't love me." She said it quietly. "That's all there is to it."

"I'm sorry, babes."

"Yeah, well. You win some, you lose some." A bitter laugh slipped out before she could stop it.

"Look, there's someone out there for you. Maybe you should give *Mr. Hot Stuff* to see if it's more than just a bedroom thing, any guy who leaves you looking like *that* after one night? He's worth exploring. Hell, I wish I could find that."

Aurora unconsciously raised a hand to her cheek. Did she look that different after just one night? "I don't think I'm ready to see anyone, honestly. I —" She stopped short, biting back the flood of words that almost spilled out.

"I didn't get his number or last name no clue where he lives, he might've just been passing through. But he knows where to find me, so if he wants to see me again, it's in his hands."

Renee gave her a look, her face pinched with concern, but instead of pressing the issue, she popped another donut into her mouth. Instantly, her expression shifted to pure bliss. "See, all I've got to give me that *glow* is this box of carbs."

Aurora couldn't help but laugh, grateful for the shift in tone. The tension from the conversation seemed to ease, like a weight lifting off her chest. "I think I'll stick with that too," she said, but even as she spoke, she knew the truth. If Malik showed up at her door tonight, she'd let him in and probably the night after that.

Damn, she thought, *I'm so screwed.*

...

"I need a status report from you."

Malik shrugged, barely glancing at his superior. Ordog was lounging in his oversized, throne-like chair, surrounded by piles of ancient scrolls and dusty tomes. The whole scene looked like something out of the Dark Ages, not the seat of a powerful demon.

"No deadlines looming. Everything's under control," he said, casually.

"Is it?"

He fell silent, waiting. He knew what was coming. He'd been slacking off, and Ordog wasn't the type to let that slide unnoticed.

"I've noticed your workload has become… lighter," he continued, his tone deceptively calm. "Far fewer cases than any of the others. Care to explain why you've gotten so *lazy*?"

"Would it make a difference if I did?" Malik said with a sigh, his patience already fraying.

Ordog just stared the silence thickening with tension. Malik forced himself to keep talking. "I've never been much for defending myself. It's not like it's worked in my favor before."

"What's going on with you, Malik? Burned out?"

"Maybe."

"Or is it something else? Perhaps your attention has been... diverted elsewhere? Say, somewhere it shouldn't have been last night?"

Shit... Busted. Malik's eyes flicked to the looking glass in the corner of the room Ordog's surveillance system. If you stared into it long enough, it would show you the location of any demon on the surface and what they were up to. Malik had underestimated just how closely he was being watched. Being one of the oldest and most trusted collectors had made him complacent... that trust was wearing thin.

"Is there a problem?" he asked, choosing his words carefully. It was smart to tread lightly. One wrong step, and he could easily end up on the wrong side of Ordog's torture dungeon—or worse.

Ordog leaned forward, casually flipping open one of the thick tomes on his lap. A piece of parchment slipped out and fluttered to the ground, but he didn't notice. Malik bent down and picked it up, his eyes skimming the words scrawled across it in his superior's nearly illegible handwriting:

"You shall cleanse the abomination, cast out the afflicted, for it is an offense too vile for even Hell to endure."

Malik frowned, unfamiliar with the decree. *What kind of offense is so bad that even Hell won't tolerate it?* Whatever it was, it had to be rare. He opened his mouth to ask, but Ordog interrupted him.

"I'll take that," he said, hand outstretched, his eyes narrowing dangerously.

Malik handed it over without hesitation. Whatever it was, it wasn't his business. It's probably some top-secret head demon bullshit.

He tucked the parchment back into the book, then leaned back. "Now, as for you... My records show that your contract with Andreas Rayner for the soul of Aurora DeBorealis remains open-ended. You've had plenty of time to move on this why haven't you collected?"

Malik fought the urge to roll his eyes. "Because it's *open-ended*," he said slowly, as if explaining something painfully obvious to a child. "I'm biding my time, choosing my moment."

"And you didn't find that moment last night?"

His jaw clenched. "What difference does it make? Whether I take her now or years from now, she's ours."

It was the lie he'd been telling himself since Aurora had kissed the tips of his fingers when they'd hovered over her heart, ready to claim her soul. He didn't need to rush there'd be other chances.

"I'm telling you to take her now."

Malik froze.

Ordog continued, his voice sharp. "We can't afford to wait. Every day you delay is a day those insufferable golden morons could interfere. The fact that I have to remind you of this... is troubling. You used to be one of my best, Malik. Quick, efficient. Why are you dragging your feet now?"

He stared at the floor, forcing his face to remain blank. He had been ready to strike. Last night. He'd prepared himself to take her until she'd looked at him with those blue eyes until her lips had brushed against his fingers, her kiss soft and innocent.

" Malakiás!"

His gaze snapped back to Ordog, who was watching him with eyes the color of molten sulfur. "Don't let something as trivial as lust distract you from your purpose. She's a human, nothing more. I trust you won't let your baser instincts interfere with your duty."

He forced a nod. "Of course not."

"Good. Then go back and finish the job. I don't want to have to send someone else." The threat in Ordog's voice was unmistakable.

He gritted his teeth. He'd had what he wanted from her just one night, that's all it had been. Ordog was right, it was dangerous to linger delaying only increased the risk of some divine intervention. He'd learned that the hard way.

He wasn't supposed to care about anything else. All that mattered was claiming what was his. But when he thought about Aurora, her soft warmth, the way her lips had parted under his, the way she had *trusted* him, he couldn't shake the feeling that maybe, for the first time, he did care.

And that was a problem.

Chapter 8

Aurora loved working at Renee's store. That wasn't work, it was getting paid to hang out with friends, talk about books, and laugh all day. It always lifted her mood, no matter what was weighing on her mind.

But her serving job? That was another story entirely.

Sure, she tried not to complain—at least she had a second job. The place was upscale, the tips were decent, and she could always find something else if it came to that. But while she hadn't quite hit her breaking point, she knew it was lurking just beyond the next miserable shift. She was toughing it out for now.

Still, it felt far worse when they called her in on her night off. And tonight? Well, tonight stung even more because this place, the one she despised, was where she'd first met James.

He'd been here on some business lunch, all buttoned-up and charming. She'd been nervous, fumbling through a busy afternoon, and spilled a glass of water on his shirt. How ironic that the very clumsiness he'd eventually leave her over was what first caught his attention. She could still remember he'd lingered at the table while the rest of his party moved toward the door, how he gently grabbed her wrist as she passed by, slipping her his business card.

She'd grinned like a fool for the rest of the day.

Now, the memory left a bitter taste in her mouth. **Of course**, he'd made her come to him. Jerk off.

She could've said no when they'd called her to work tonight, but she wasn't stupid enough to turn down the money. And honestly, sitting alone at home didn't sound much better. That would give her too much time to think, she already knew where those thoughts would take her hoping for a knock at the door that would never come.

Now, here she was, clad in her pressed white shirt, black slacks, and the small apron tied around her waist carrying her notepad, serving all the happy, carefree couples on their Saturday night dates. She couldn't help but imagine dumping a glass of red wine into their smug, smiling laps. It was a small comfort, even if it was just a fantasy.

For someone who had been so frantic to get in touch with her last night, James hadn't bothered today. She gnawed on her lip, barely listening as she scribbled down the latest convoluted order. Her thoughts swirled. Did he know what she'd done? Why did she even care?

There was no chance of reconciliation. James was as stubborn as they came. When he made up his mind it was like a switch had been flipped—permanent. Unchangeable. So, whatever she'd done last night didn't matter. They were done.

She pushed through the kitchen's swinging doors, dodging a waiter balancing a heavy tray on his shoulder. The manager was shouting in a high-pitched screech that grated on her nerves. She barely registered the words as she refilled her water pitcher and left. Her feet ached, her head pounded and the blissful afterglow of last night's reckless decisions had faded.

She wasn't even sure which hurt more—losing James or Malik.

What did that say about her? How messed up was she?

She needed a break. Glancing at the clock, she yelled "Break!" and made a beeline for the bathroom. The walls felt like they were closing in, and the bathroom wasn't much better, but at least it was quiet. At least she could breathe.

Cool water splashed onto her face. She let it drip down her cheeks, but it did nothing to cleanse the guilt or shame swirling inside her. She stared into the mirror, her reflection ghostly under the harsh fluorescent lights.

Then she saw it... Gray and hollow-eyed stared back at her from the mirror, mouth open in a silent scream as a withered hand reached for her shoulder.

She gasped, stumbling backward until her back hit the nearest stall. She blinked. Nothing. The reflection was normal again.

It never happened outside the house... Never.

Her nightmare was invading her waking world.

Her pulse thundered in her ears. **Get it together.** The panic attack hit like a freight train, and she slid to the floor, gasping for air. Her heart raced, her chest tight. She didn't care anymore—about anything. She was unraveling, completely losing her mind, but at least that meant the fear would finally... go away.

The bathroom door swung open, and footsteps approached, she didn't even bother getting up. If she had any fight left in her, she would have scrambled to her feet, pulled herself together, and pretended to be okay but she wasn't.

Maria, one of the other waitresses, turned the corner and stopped dead, staring at her slumped against the wall.

"You okay, love?" Marie's voice was cautious, a mix of concern and hesitation.

She nodded, though she knew exactly how she must look. Pale, shaking out of control and she still didn't care. Her face tingled with numbness as she forced her lips to move, wrenching the words from a throat that felt impossibly tight. "Just... give me a minute."

"You sure? Do I need to call—"

"I said give me a fucking minute. Please." The words came out harsher than she intended, but she didn't have the energy to apologize.

Maria's eyes flickered with something unreadable before she stomped out of the room without another word.

She clambered to her feet, her legs trembling violently, her pulse still hammering. She splashed more water on her face too much this time soaking her shirt, but it didn't matter. As soon as her hands covered her face, the tears came.

Her sobs were sharp, and uncontrollable, tearing through her like a storm she couldn't escape.

In the back of her mind, a rational voice tried to soothe her, to tell her it was fine, that she was still here, that nothing had changed. But the black pit of dread deep inside her had been spreading, growing for as long as she could remember widening, ready to consume her whole. **Those** things, the skeletal hands that haunted her dreams were going to come for her, and this time, they wouldn't let go. They'd drag her down into whatever dark, twisted place they came from, and she wasn't sure she'd even fight back when they did.

Something evil had a hold on her.

Five minutes later, she emerged from the bathroom, her hair hastily fixed, her face mostly dry. She'd patched herself together as best as she could, but the faint tremor in her hands remained, and weakness still lapped at her legs. She could feel the rawness of her emotions just under the surface, but she was determined to push through. She had no choice.

She found Maria by the kitchen door. "Thanks," she muttered, followed quickly by a shaky, "Sorry."

Maria shrugged. "Fine, whatever." She wasn't unkind, just indifferent, which was somehow worse.

She glanced toward the kitchen, where her manager was rampaging again, his shrill voice carrying through the space like nails on a chalkboard. She grabbed her water pitcher and pushed through the swinging doors, eager to avoid his gaze.

As she walked into the dining room, Peggy, the hostess, breezed by with her usual too-perky grin. "Just sat you a couple," she chirped. "Thanks."

She barely managed a nod. Hopefully, after this table, the night would start to wind down. She was beyond done.

Maybe a glass of wine afterward would help dull the sharp edges of her nerves and drown out the impending doom that seemed to hang over her like a storm cloud.

But then she saw them.

Peggy's "couple."

She froze mid-step, so suddenly that the waiter behind her collided with her back, nearly sending his tray crashing to the floor.

"Jesus, Aurora! Watch out!" he snapped, but she barely registered his voice. His tray miraculously stayed upright, but her water pitcher wasn't as lucky. The jostle sent it tilting, and before she could react, ice-cold water splashed down the back of the woman sitting right in front of her.

The woman screeched, an awful, high-pitched sound through the entire restaurant. Heads turned, curious eyes locking onto the scene. Aurora's heart pounded in her chest, but it wasn't the woman's shriek or the mess she'd made that had her paralyzed.

It was **James**.

Sitting on the other side of the restaurant, beneath the large bay windows ... he wasn't alone.

Across from him sat a woman with blonde hair. They looked relaxed and casual like, this wasn't strange at all.

Her pulse raced as her eyes locked on him. The room spun, and for a second, it felt like she might pass out. The screeching woman in front of her was still yelling, her voice growing louder, but all Aurora could focus on was James. Sitting there with that woman, his smile easy, his hand resting on the table like it belonged there.

Her throat tightened, and her hands trembled so badly she thought she might drop the empty pitcher. She had no idea how long she stood there, staring, heartbroken and furious before she finally found her feet and forced herself to move.

What the fuck?

James **knew** she worked here. What kind of asshole brought his date the day after breaking up to the workplace of the woman he'd been with for months?

To be fair not that the word should even apply, he had looked as mortified as she felt. Maybe he thought she wasn't working tonight. He knew her schedule well enough, but schedules changed all the time. He should have known that.

Now she sat in her manager's office, enduring an ass-chewing over her clumsiness every harsh word was a mirror to the way James had made her feel.

"Get your shit together, Aurora. Quit fucking everything up, Aurora. You're going to end up just like your mother, Aurora."

A cold chill lanced through her, making her sit straighter in the chair. Her boss hadn't said that. **David** had never said that. It was her voice in her head, twisting every painful memory into a sharp blade.

Could it be true? Could she end up like her mother? She'd always wondered what had driven her down that path. The thought of those same skeletal hands that haunted her nightmares dragged her down too it was enough to raise the hairs on the back of her neck if someone had offered her a syringe full of blissful emptiness, she wasn't sure she could have turned it down.

I'll never do that. She chanted it to herself, over and over. **I'll never be her.**

Her boss finally sent her home, probably thanks to Maria spilling the details about her breakdown earlier. They all probably thought she was on the verge of a nervous collapse and honestly, they wouldn't be far off. At least she didn't have to see James again. She ducked out the back, avoiding the dining room where **he** and that woman were sitting.

The image of her burned in her mind. The woman had been tall, even seated. Her toned arms and long legs gave her a sleek, polished look. Everything about her was perfect, from her glittering dress to her matching red lips which curled in amused pity when she spilled that water.

She's everything I'm not.

She shook the thought away and made for her car. If only she had Malik's number, she'd be calling him. She needed him tonight to lick her wounds, to make her forget. To make her scream and obliterate everything that was hurting her.

Just as she reached her car, she heard footsteps rushing behind her. She hurried to open the door, but before she could jump inside... James grabbed her arm and the car door, blocking her escape.

"Aurora, please, just give me two minutes. Let me explain."

"Fuck you."

"Don't be like that—"

"To hell with you! Isn't that what you said to me last night? What am I supposed to be like, James? Oh, I get it now. You're an asshole. Now let me go before I start screaming."

"It's not what it looks like, I promise—"

Her heart pounded in her ears. She saw red. "You don't have a sister or any close female friends I know of, so don't try to spin me some lie. You brought **her** here."

"I thought you were off tonight!" He ran a hand through his hair, glancing at the distant traffic. "And this is where she wanted to go."

Her jaw clenched so hard it hurt. The betrayal was suffocating. Her body tense with the need to claw at him, to scream, to make him hurt like she was hurting, but she forced herself to stay still. If she moved, she might lose control completely. "How long, James? Who is she?"

"Aurora—"

"Tell me!"

"She works in my building. I've known her for two months, but I swear I never cheated on you. Tonight is the first time we've been out together."

"Bullshit."

His mouth set in a firm line. "What reason do I have to lie to you now? If I'd been sleeping with her, I'd tell you. But it doesn't matter, does it? You won't believe me either way."

"So, you weren't fucking her, but you wanted to. Oh, I feel **so** much better now."

"If you can't be an adult about this—"

Her temper flared. "Adult? You don't know how badly I want to slap you right now. I thought you were better than this, James."

His eyes narrowed, dark with barely controlled rage. "You didn't seem so broken up about it last night. Not enough to stop you from spreading your legs for some stranger."

His words were venomous, and they struck her like a blow to the chest. Her breath caught, the retort dying on her lips as her mind whirled. **He'd seen her.**

"I watched you leave with him, Aurora. I followed because I thought you were giving him a ride, but no. I called because I was worried about you. You don't even know that guy."

His mouth twisted bitterly. "I guess your mouth was too occupied to answer."

She was trembling. His words were like knives stabbing at her heart. He was shredding her, and he knew it.

"So don't stand here acting all insulted because I'm moving on. You've got me beat by a mile."

She choked back her response, her voice barely a whisper. "That's rich, coming from someone who couldn't wait to get in her pants while we were still together."

"At least I ended things with you first."

"Yeah, you're a real gentleman, James. Go away and don't come back to my restaurant."

He smirked, but it wasn't the smile she used to love. It was twisted and ugly. "After tonight, it might not be your restaurant for long."

Her stomach twisted, and the hurt too much to bear. But just as she was about to respond, a new voice cut through the tension.

"I believe, I heard the lady ask you to leave her alone."

Malik stepped from around the car. His face was hard, his posture rigid. James straightened to his full height, but she barely noticed. All she could think was how Malik looked stronger, more imposing.

James's voice wavered as he tried to hold his ground. "This is a private conversation."

Malik's voice, low and steady, held no room for argument. "It's over."

Her pulse quickened. She knew James didn't respond well to threats and could sense Malik wasn't the type to back down. Panic clawed at her chest this could get ugly.

"He's right," she interjected, stepping between them. "We're done here, James. You made your choice now leave me alone."

James's jaw tightened, but he finally looked away from Malik, his eyes softening as they landed on her. "Yeah. Fine." He threw one last, hateful glance at Malik before stalking back toward the restaurant.

Aurora watched him go, numbness settling in her chest like a weight. Numb was good, it was easier than feeling.

Malik moved to her side, his presence comforting in a way she didn't want to acknowledge just yet. "Another embarrassing moment you've witnessed," she said, tipping her head back to meet his gaze. "What are you doing here?"

His lips quirked at the corner. "I've been following you."

She raised an eyebrow. "Really?"

He laughed softly. "Kidding. I was leaving the bar and saw you. Lucky timing, I guess."

"More than a little," she muttered. "You weren't with a date, were you?"

"After you? No one would compare."

She rolled her eyes, but deep down, his words tugged at something vulnerable inside her.

Before she could respond, Malik's expression shifted. His gaze hardened, staring past her, focused on something she couldn't see.

"What is it?" she asked, turning to follow his line of sight.

But all she saw was the parking lot and the freeway beyond it.

When she turned back to him, his face was set in a way that sent a shiver up her spine.

"Malik?"

He blinked, shaking his head like he was snapping out of a trance. "What?" he asked, his voice distant.

"What, what? What do you see?" she demanded, her voice tight, pulse still racing from the confrontation with James. Malik's sudden shift in demeanor unnerved her, and she wasn't sure if it was just her nerves from earlier or something else entirely.

"Nothing," he said, his eyes clearing as he brushed it off. "So where are you going now?"

"Home." She paused, swallowing down the question that almost slipped out. **Do you want to come?** She didn't want to ask. She shouldn't. She knew she was already treading into dangerous territory with this guy. His presence unnerved her more than she liked to admit. He'd been on her mind all day, a constant pulse she couldn't shake. And now? Now, just standing this close to him had her thighs clenching, trying to quell the ache building inside her.

Her breasts felt heavy, her nipples straining against the fabric of her bra, craving his touch. She could barely keep herself together, her body betraying her in ways she hadn't felt since... well, since the night before. She should be heartbroken over James. She should have been numb and disconnected part of her was, but the rest wanted him... Badly.

She tried to resist the pull, but it was futile. The urge to drag him into her car and lose herself in him, right there in the parking lot, was overwhelming.

When he slammed her back against her car and kissed her, her resolve disintegrated. The heat of his mouth on hers, the sheer intensity of his kiss, made her knees buckle.

"Shit," she gasped against his lips, breathless. He chuckled softly, the sound vibrating against her skin. She'd forgotten about his heat and how being near him made her feel like she was on fire.

He pulled her shirt free from her pants, his hand sliding up to cup her breast. She gasped again, biting back a giggle.

"What's so funny?" he murmured, his voice thick with desire but laced with amusement.

"You just... you make me happy, and I needed that right now." She said the words before she could stop herself. The moment they left her lips, she regretted it.

He paused, his hand slipping from her breast, his eyes searching her face. Hell. She hadn't meant it like **that**.

She opened her mouth to backtrack, to explain, but he silenced her with a finger against her lips.

"Shh. It's all right." His voice was calm and steady. "It's just... the first time anyone's ever said that to me."

Her heart twisted. How had no one ever told him that before? What kind of women had he known? She'd only known him a day, but something about him intrigued her in ways that felt far too dangerous. The tattoos, the mystery, the way he made her feel so alive, it pulled her in.

That thought quickly faded as she imagined his tattoos shifting over his muscles, flexing under her fingers. The mere idea sent a slow burn through her veins, making her light-headed with desire.

"Are we going to stand here all night," she breathed, slipping her fingers through his belt loops and grinding her hips into him, "or are we going to do something about this?"

His hands traveled up to her cheeks, forcing her to look into his eyes. His touch sent sparks through her, and she sucked in a sharp breath. "Now there's an invitation I can't resist," he murmured.

Her lips twisted bitterly for a moment, her emotions catching up with her lust. "Even though I'm such a fucking mess?"

He smiled softly, brushing his thumb over her bottom lip. "But such a pretty mess," he replied. His voice dropped, sending shivers down her spine. "I do have to take care of something first, though. Why don't you head to your place, and I'll meet you there in thirty minutes?"

Disappointment flared in her chest, but she quickly tamped it down. "Okay. Are you sure? If it's bad timing—"

"It is... dreadful timing." He smiled again, softer this time. "But I'm still going to be with you. What does that tell you?"

The answer hit her square in the chest. **This is more than just a distraction.** This thing between them was heading straight for her heart, and she knew it. She was falling fast, and part of her wanted to slam the brakes. But another part of her that craved him wasn't about to stop it.

"Okay," she whispered, nodding.

As he stepped back, she couldn't resist giving him one last look, her eyes tracing the lines of his face. He was troubled she could feel it but for now, he was the trouble she needed.

She got into her car and started the engine, her body still buzzing from his touch. As she pulled out of the parking lot, she glanced in the rearview mirror, watching him as he stood there, motionless, watching her leave.

What had he seen earlier? And what was he about to take care of?

Questions swirled in her mind, but none mattered as much as the one thing she couldn't deny: she wasn't about to stop whatever this was between them.

Not yet.

Chapter 9

Once Malik had tucked Aurora into her car, given her one last lingering kiss, and shut the door, he stood still, watching the taillights disappear into the night. Only when it vanished did he turn to face the God who'd intruded so rudely the same one who'd cornered him last night.

"Well?" Malik demanded, arms crossed.

"You have an appointment," Sol replied, calm and detached.

He scoffed. "You've got that right."

"Not with her," he said, his voice a low murmur. "With the mediator."

Malik's gut twisted. Fuck! How had the bastard managed that? The deal was airtight. "Why bother?"

"I asked myself the same thing," Sol replied, pulling a scroll from his robes and tossing it at Malik's feet. "But, better safe than sorry. You've been stayed pending our meeting with Minos."

Malik stared, fury building. "You're kidding."

"Until then," he continued, unfazed, "you're barred from claiming her." His mouth curled into a slight, smug smile. "Not that I think I needed it, but you're hanging around a bit too much. I figured your superiors would get nervous sooner or later. You're all so… unpredictable."

"You cryptic bastard," Malik growled. "What's that supposed to mean?"

The God's smile grew sharper. "You're delusional if you can't figure it out." With that, he turned, shooting up toward the sky, swift as a comet.

Malik stared after him, then down at the scroll. He picked it up and unfurled it, giving it only a glance. Everything looked in order—no way to move on Aurora now. His fists clenched at his sides.

But even as anger simmered, something unexpected crept in. **Relief.** The realization rocked him he didn't have to worry about her tonight. No contract, no duty. Just her. Just him.

When had he started worrying?

The thought of being with her, unburdened, sent a shiver through him. It was thrilling and terrifying. The enormity of the feeling shook him to the core. No duty. Just pleasure.

How would it feel to spend a night without the weight of that contract looming over them? The promise of eternity should have been enough. It should bring him peace, but all he could think about was her, waiting for him, probably already home, thinking of him, anticipating their night together.

True peace would come once the contract was sealed, once her soul was his forever. Yet, he couldn't summon more than mild irritation at the God. Instead, all his thoughts turned toward the night ahead.

He paced the parking lot, watching couples walk hand-in-hand, their laughter floating in the cool night air. For the first time in his long, fractured existence, Malik knew exactly how they felt.

...

Her door flew open before Malik even had time to knock. She stood there, eyes wide, practically bouncing with excitement. Her enthusiasm hit him like a wave, and he found himself grinning despite everything.

"Okay," she blurted before he could even say hello. "You can say no if you want but my friend called, and when I told her I was off early and, um, seeing you... she asked if we wanted to meet her for a few drinks at this club downtown. I just thought... maybe it would be fun. Dancing, if you like that sort of thing. If not, that's cool too. I said I'd ask. That's all."

He couldn't stop grinning at her nervous energy, the way she rambled without even taking a breath. Dancing. He didn't dance. But if it made her this excited, he could pretend. "Sure. We can do that."

Her whole face lit up, and she bounced again. "Awesome! But first, will you tell me one thing?"

"Anything."

"What's your last name?" she asked, biting her lower lip as if she was embarrassed by the question.

Malik raised an eyebrow, all the things she could ask, that was it? "Samael," he said, thinking quickly. "Malik Samael."

"Samael." She tested the name on her tongue, then smiled. "Malik Samael and I'm Aurora DeBorealis just, you know, in case you were wondering."

He took her hand and lifted it to his lips. "Charmed, Aurora DeBorealis." And he was. Far more than he should have been.

Her cheeks flushed as she gave a soft laugh pulling him inside and shutting the door behind them. "So... do you live here?" she asked, leading him further into the apartment.

"No. I don't," he replied, watching her reaction closely. He saw her face fall, only for a moment, before she masked it with a smile.

"Oh. Okay," she said lightly, but her curiosity wasn't easily dismissed. "Where are you from, then?"

"Here and there," he said, knowing it wasn't enough. He hesitated, then added, "I move a lot."

"That sounds interesting," she said, heading toward her bedroom. "I'll just be a minute—I'm going to change."

"Take your time," He muttered, mentally cursing himself. He sounded like an ass. "I live in Florida right now," he added quickly.

Her voice floated from the other room. "Really? I never would've guessed! You don't sound like you're from the south, but I guess you wouldn't since you moved so much.

He couldn't help but smirk. "Yeah. I'm here on business."

"The contract stuff you don't like to talk about, huh?"

"Something like that," he muttered, his thoughts interrupted when she reappeared, reaching up to adjust his jacket zipper. The casual intimacy of the gesture made his chest tighten. He was supposed to be distant and detached, yet every small touch felt like it anchored him deeper to her.

She looked up at him apologetically. "I'm sorry. I don't mean to press for your life story. I knew what was up when I brought you here last night, and now I'm acting like we're..."

Her words trailed off as her fingers lingered on his jacket. "I'll stop, okay? You tell me what you want when you want. If you want."

He looked down at her, taking in the shy yet direct gaze and the quiet vulnerability behind it. She would be any mortal man's dream, yet here she was waiting for him... trusting him.

"The truth is, Aurora..." He hesitated, then continued, "I'm only in town for a couple of weeks."

She nodded, trying to appear nonchalant. "I get it."

"No, it's... complicated," he said, gently brushing a curl from her forehead. His fingertips lingered against her warm skin, sensing the lingering fear she'd been hiding. Something had happened tonight, something that still haunted her.

"But if it's all right with you," he said softly, "I wouldn't mind your company while I'm here."

"It's all right with me," she replied, but he could hear the slight sadness in her voice or maybe he was just listening for it. "So, we'll just... have fun while you're here?"

"Sounds like a plan," he agreed, though his mind was racing with thoughts far darker than she could ever imagine.

She smiled, and something deep within him broke. How the hell could he take her now, knowing this? For the first time in his existence, he entertained the thought of thanking Minos for the delay. Because there was no way in Hell he could have claimed her tonight, not after that smile.

Maybe, just maybe, he was beginning to wonder if he could take her at all.

...

"Well, he can't dance," Renee yelled over the pounding bass, "but he's hot enough to make up for it."

Aurora giggled, taking another sip of her red wine. Malik had drifted off toward the men's room giving her and Renee a moment alone at their table. The dance floor pulsed with bodies, the club lights flashing in time with the music, but the sense of excitement Aurora had felt earlier was beginning to dull.

"Oh, he's not that bad," she said trying to sound casual.

Renee arched an eyebrow. "Not that bad? If he's got the moves to put the look on your face that I saw this morning, there might be hope for him yet."

She blushed, twirling her glass on its thin coaster. "Not that it matters. He told me he's leaving in two weeks."

Renee rolled her eyes. "So?"

"So… he made it pretty clear this is just a fling. I'm okay with that."

Renee's expression darkened, her smoky eyes narrowing. "No, you're not."

She shrugged. "Well… it's better than nothing, right? Two weeks of fun, no strings attached."

Renee leaned in closer. "So is a vibrator. Sometimes, a big dick comes with a bigger headache."

She laughed, but the sound didn't reach her eyes. "Don't do that, If I didn't agree to this I wouldn't be here."

"Yeah, but here's the thing you say you're okay now, but I've seen this before, Aur. You're already daydreaming about more."

Her smile faltered, her gaze falling to the table. "I'm just trying to live in the moment."

Renee sighed, reaching out to squeeze her wrist. "I get it. I just don't want you getting hurt. Again."

"All right, look. I don't mean to rain on your parade."

Aurora shook her head. "No, if you weren't exactly right, then I wouldn't be upset."

"I don't want to be right," Renee said. "And yes, I was cheering for the guy this morning, but I don't like him arranging with you where he gets his jollies for a couple of weeks, and you're left picking up the pieces again after he's gone. I want you to get whatever you want out of this deal. But I see the little wheels spinning already, and I'm afraid that you'll end up wanting the white picket fences and there's nothing wrong with that. It's just that you keep looking for them in the wrong places."

Aurora laughed. "So, what you're saying is you think I have zero chance of making him fall madly in love with me in two weeks?" She allowed a sly little grin as she asked it.

Renee pointed two fingers at her. "A-ha. Caught ya." Aurora shoved her playfully, and her friend went on. "He'd be a fool not to, sweetie. I know that, and you know that…"

"Right. Here he comes."

Renee kept up a stream of chatter and witticisms with Malik despite the unsavory nature of her and Aurora's prior conversation about him. Bless her. But the flashing lights and pulsing music were beginning to wear on her nerves, and before long she and Malik were saying good night. Renee hugged her and slinked her way back onto the dance floor.

As they strolled down the sidewalk, Aurora breathed in the cool night air, trying to shake off Renee's words. The rhythmic pulse of the club faded behind them, replaced by the hum of distant traffic and the occasional shouts from a nearby alley.

For a while, they walked in comfortable silence, their fingers intertwined. But as the street grew quieter, she felt a prickle of unease. The storefronts they passed had become dingier, the buildings older, some marred by graffiti and cracked windows.

"Hey," she said, glancing around. "I didn't realize how far we'd gone. We should head back. This area..."

"As long as you're with me, you don't have to worry about it," he said, squeezing her hand.

"Cocky, aren't we?" She tried to smile, but the strange tension in the air was gnawing at her.

He chuckled, turning them around. "All right. Let's head back."

They'd barely taken a few steps when a figure stepped out from the shadows ahead of them. Aurora's heart stuttered. Her worst nightmare had just materialized. Well, one of them.

The man was gaunt, his face pale under the streetlight, his eyes hollow and wild. A gun glinted in his trembling hand, pointed directly at them.

"Gimme your wallet, man, and the bitch's purse," he snarled, his voice raspy.

Aurora's entire body froze, her breath catching in her throat. She clutched Malik's arm, her gaze locked on the gun. This was how it happened—this was how she'd die.

But beside her, Malik didn't even flinch.

He took a step forward, his voice low, almost a growl. "Get out of our way before I waste you."

Aurora's stomach dropped. Was he insane? She tugged at his arm, whispering frantically, "Malik, just give him what he wants—"

He caught her wrist before she could move, his grip firm but calm. "I've got this," he muttered under his breath.

"You better listen to her, man," the mugger said, brandishing the gun. "I ain't playin'."

Malik's eyes darkened, and something in his expression shifted, becoming almost... predatory. "Neither am I call her a bitch again, and I'll make you regret it."

The mugger blinked, taking a step back. His hand was shaking, the gun trembling in his grip.

"Back off," he continued, his voice low and menacing. "Those shakes are rough, huh? You couldn't hit either of us if you tried."

The gun snapped up, pointing directly at Malik's face. "Keep talkin', man, and I'll show you a bullet up close and personal."

Aurora's heart pounded in her ears. Oh God, this is it. He's going to shoot him.

But Malik didn't even blink. He stepped closer, his voice steady and calm. "You can't afford bullets, can you?

Even if you could, it won't be enough. You'll never be able to feed the beast inside you."

The mugger's eyes widened, flickering with panic. His hand shook violently, the gun wavering. He was losing control, and Malik was pushing him closer to the edge.

"What the fuck's wrong with you, man?" the mugger growled, desperation creeping into his voice.

"Walk away," he said, his voice a low command. "Before you do something stupid."

The man's face twisted in rage, and Aurora saw the moment he snapped, his finger tightening on the trigger.

"Fuck you!" he screamed, and the gun exploded, the deafening crack of the shot echoing off the buildings.

Chapter 10

Brushing one's teeth with someone else nibbling at one's neck was hard. Aurora giggled and swatted at him, dislodging a bit of toothpaste foam from her mouth. Despite her squealing efforts to catch it, the foam dribbled down the front of her black nightshirt.

She dabbed at the spot with her free hand, pulling the toothbrush from her mouth. "Ah! Look what you did."

"How tragic," he replied with a smirk, already strolling out of the bathroom, his work done.

"I'm going to get you for that," she called after him. "Now I'm stained for the night."

"As if you're going to be wearing it for long," he teased from the bedroom.

A shiver of anticipation ran through her. Nearly a week had passed since the incident on the street, and he had come over every night. Every night, he'd given her the best orgasm of her life. Frighteningly enough, it only seemed to get better.

She didn't know what was happening between them, but she wasn't complaining. How could she? The sex was astronomical—each touch sent her floating somewhere around Venus.

But still, there was that uncertainty not once had he mentioned what would happen after his two weeks were up. She was between elation when they were together and quiet dread when they weren't. It probably wasn't good for her, but hell when had anything in her life been different? Tonight, she wouldn't let the worries ruin their time together.

Grinning at her reflection, she leaned over the sink to rinse out her mouth—and froze, her scream caught in her throat.

Blood gushed from the faucet, red and vivid against the white porcelain. It covered her hands, dripping between her fingers and splattering onto the countertop. She jerked back, choking on her breath as she stared at her hands—both drenched in the slick red liquid.

She stumbled, her heart pounding in her chest. A glimpse in the mirror made her reel further: a gray face, twisted in agony, silently screamed at her from the glass.

Her scream finally tore free.

Whirling around, she slammed her back against the counter. Nothing was there. The faucet ran clear again, the water harmlessly swirling down the drain.

Malik appeared in the doorway, his brow furrowed as he took in her wide eyes and trembling form.

"Are you okay?" he asked, his gaze raking over her from bare feet to her pale face. She knew she must look like death itself—she always did after one of her episodes.

Normally, she'd fake composure or break down completely. This time, her voice came out broken, shaky. "Will I ever get used to it?"

"Get used to what?" he asked, stepping closer.

"After all these years... you'd think, I'd get used to it. But I don't. Every time I see something, it's as bad as the first time."

He moved into the room, taking her trembling hands in his. His grip was warm, steady. "What did you see?"

She glanced down at the pristine white sink, struggling to control her breath. "It was running with blood. And... the faces. In the mirror. I saw them again, Malik. I saw them the other night at the restaurant, too. It's never happened outside wherever I lived before. But now... it's following me."

Her voice rose with panic, and he closed the distance, pulling her into his arms. "It's going to be okay," he murmured into her hair.

"Am I losing my mind?" she whispered against the warmth of his bare shoulder.

"No," he said firmly, his voice filled with quiet certainty.

"How can you say that? What else could it be? Seeing things that aren't there—that's crazy, right? There's no other explanation—"

"Haunted," he said softly.

She pulled back just enough to look up at him, her breath catching. "Haunted? Like... a poltergeist?"

"Or worse."

She scoffed, shaking her head. "I've wished it could be something like that something I could get rid of. But honestly... I don't believe in those things."

He stared back at her, steady and assured. "After everything you've seen? How can you not? You're not crazy, Aurora. You're completely coherent."

"That doesn't matter," she muttered. "It doesn't feel that way."

He brushed a strand of hair back from her face with both hands, his touch gentle. "It looks that way. You're strong."

"Strong?" her brow furrowed. No one had ever described her as strong. What was wrong with him? "That's the last word I'd use to describe me."

"No, it's the last word you think others would use to describe you... people like your ex but forget about them. Even if you don't believe me about being haunted, believe me when I say you are not weak, and you are not crazy."

She stared at him, her heart still racing. "So... let's say you're right and this thing is following me... how do I get rid of it? It's been with me since I was a little girl, no matter where I live. It's after me."

His gaze darkened slightly as he regarded her. "But you're still here."

His words hung in the air, cryptic and calm. He said it as if he were trying to solve some puzzle, though it was the same thought she'd clung to all these years to keep herself together. His eyes flicked around the room before settling back on her.

"Are you done here? Let's go to bed," he said quietly.

She turned off the faucet, allowing him to guide her out of the bathroom, but not without casting one last glance at the mirror. All she saw was her face, pale and shadowed—haunted.

"The first time I remember it… really remember it… I was thirteen," she said softly. They were lying face-to-face, their fingers intertwined, the room bathed in the soft shadows of night. "Things had happened before that, but they were minor. Infrequent but on my thirteenth birthday, I saw the faces for the first time."

He listened intently as her gaze drifted past him, far away, her voice tinged with the weight of old memories.

"My grandmother had a party for me I spent the whole time curled up in my bedroom, crying. She couldn't get me to come out I guess that's why I never got another party. I think they had the same problem most people do she was scared shitless of me."

He could almost understand. Sometimes, he was scared shitless of her too.

"It was worse in the beginning," she continued, her voice growing distant. "I tried to hide it from everyone. My family, the few friends I had. I didn't look in a mirror for years I avoided them whenever I could."

"You seem to now," he said gently.

Her eyes met his, but he knew she wasn't seeing him. "I forced myself to care. When I was seventeen, this guy I liked started showing interest, and I wanted to be normal. I tried to pretend none of it was happening for him, for myself but it didn't last. Guys came and went, and I kept hiding it, until James. I thought we were close enough that he could handle it, but he couldn't." She sighed, her fingers tightening around his. "I can't blame him, though it's not his fault."

His jaw tightened. "Can you blame him for being a coward who deserted you? Yeah, pretty easily."

She let out a small laugh. "I guess so." She paused, her voice softer now. "But it's better to let it go. I got so tired of being afraid all the time and I still do. Some days I feel defiant, like I can beat it. Other days... I'm a mess."

Defiant, she could be, he thought. He'd seen her strength, even if she didn't recognize it. She had always been beyond his reach until now and he'd had to exploit someone else's weakness to get to her.

He had come close once, long ago, or at least, closer than he had in centuries. She'd been hung as a witch in some in Salem when all she'd done was ease women through the rigors of childbirth. He could still remember the nobleman's wife had died in childbirth despite all of her efforts, and that was all it took for them to turn on her.

They called her a witch, the devil's handmaid, consorting with demons. If only they had known how close to the truth they were.

He had revealed himself to her the night before her execution, in that cold, dank cell. Desperation had driven him, knowing he was about to lose her again. Who knew how long he would have to wait until her soul returned? If it returned at all. He'd been ready to offer anything to save her but had to tread carefully.

He could still see her, kneeling on the floor of that dark cell, her lips murmuring prayers. Even then, facing death, she had looked beautiful to him. Defiant. Unbroken. He had wanted her so badly, he could barely contain it. "If there were any way to escape your fate," he had said, gripping the bars between them, "would you take it?"

Her answer had been strong, her voice steady despite the fear in her eyes. "I would not lie to save myself nor sell my soul. I'll face the noose and find my peace in eternity before I ever face the fires of Hell."

Her rejection had filled him with rage, the fury rising in his chest until he could feel his eyes burn crimson. He had snarled at her, his final words sharp and bitter: "Shall I ask again when the air starts to leave your chest?"

"Get thee behind me, Demon!" she had cried, the words hitting him like a blow.

The next morning, he had watched her hang, his anger barely held in check. She should have been his, but the Gods had taken her, carrying her soul while one of them smirked at him before disappearing into the ice-blue sky.

Who was smirking now?

Not him. Not at the moment. He shook the memory away, focusing on the present. That was then, and this is now. He was no longer watching her from the shadows, helpless to claim her. Now, she was in his arms, in his bed, where she was wanted.

She snuggled closer against his chest, her breath cool. He was about to let her drift off to sleep she needed the rest but the memory of her down on her knees, praying, still wreaked havoc on him. His body responded, hardening with an intensity he could barely control.

As if sensing his need, she tilted her head and brushed her lips against his. Her fingers slid down to lightly stroke his cock, and every muscle in his body tightened. "Is this for me?" she teased.

He could only groan her name in reply and sink into her kiss, tasting her, plundering the mouth that had once murmured prayers, now, at last, she was his.

"Oh, Malik," she sighed, her lips brushing his.

"I love that sound, say it again?" he whispered against her skin.

She giggled, repeating his name over and over. He laughed too, nibbling at her bottom lip until the words became breathless sounds between them. He kissed down her jaw to her throat, where her pulse beat strong and fast beneath his lips.

"Thank you for listening to all my insanity," she whispered as his mouth lingered on her neck. "For understanding me you don't know how much it means…"

Her voice cracked, and he stilled, lifting his head. Tears shimmered in her eyes, and she blinked rapidly, trying to hide them.

But they belonged to a soul far more broken than she realized. Bravely, she forced the words out. "You don't know how much it means to be with someone I can say anything to. It's weird, having known you for only a week maybe that's why… no pressure. What do you think?"

Shit. Did she expect him to talk when her hand was doing that?

He looked at her face at the slight differences in this incarnation, the sharp nose, the rounded cheeks. Despite the changes, he knew her face better than his own. She was always the same. Always blue-eyed, always red-haired... always her.

"Aurora," he rasped, fighting to keep control. "I think you're incredible. I think… that's why… oh, fuck… that's why this dark entity has attached itself to you."

Her hand froze, and for a moment, he nearly whimpered. Where the hell had that come from?

"Really?" she asked, her voice quiet.

He groaned inwardly, scrambling for a response. "Well… I mean, I would."

She looked at him and then laughed a soft, easy sound that made his stomach twist. Yeah, haha. She thanked him now, trusted him now, but it wouldn't last. The day she learned the truth, she would hate him. She would curse him. **Get thee behind me, indeed.**

It shouldn't matter, but it did.

As she slid her mouth down his chest, kissing a slow, deliberate trail toward the epicenter of the erotic agony she'd stirred in him, He tangled his fingers in her hair, his breath catching he dreaded that day with everything in him.

No sense denying it any longer after all these centuries, she was here, she was his and if he weren't contractually obligated to take her soul, he wouldn't.

But he was.

And that was the cruelest part of it all.

Chapter 11

Another week passed filled with more bliss than a demon should ever know. Malik didn't get to spend every moment with her she had work, after all, but that only made the time they shared all the sweeter. Every second he spent with her was intoxicating, making him forget if only briefly, the reality of what was coming.

But tonight, that fragile fantasy was about to end.

He materialized in front of the grand old house Minos called home. For the first time in centuries, nerves clawed at him. What was going to happen here tonight? The implications of this meeting weighed heavily on him. He had to keep his mask in place. If Sol or worse, Minos saw even a glimmer of hesitation, he would never live it down. He had a reputation to uphold. A job to do, whether he liked it or not.

He stepped inside, greeted by the scent of fragrant wax and ancient tomes, the smell always too heavy with memories of past dealings... how he hated this place.

Minos and Sol were already waiting in the study, a dim, cavernous room lined with bookshelves and the source of the musty scent. He plastered on his usual air of arrogant indifference as he strolled in, his footsteps echoing across the stone floor. Both men turned to look at him.

"Minos, my old friend," he drawled, grinning as though nothing could touch him. "Aren't you nearing retirement age?"

Sol merely shook his head, but Minos gave a small nod of greeting, as formal as ever. "Your attendance and participation are appreciated."

Malik scoffed, tossing himself into one of the gilded chairs. The chair creaked under him, old enough to crumble. "It's my understanding they're required."

"You could always forfeit," Sol said, his tone mild but with an edge of satisfaction. "I wouldn't mind."

"I'm sure you wouldn't." Malik leaned back, folding his arms. "But now that the pleasantries are out of the way, let's get down to business." He pulled the contract from his jacket and tossed it onto the desk before Minos could ask. The old man unfurled it, his face betraying nothing as he read through the fine print.

"I love that this is just business to you," Sol remarked, voice low and calm, though something darker lurked beneath the surface.

Malik shot him a glance. "And what is it to you?"

"Far more than that."

"Oh, come on." Malik leaned forward, flashing a grin that masked his unease. "Are your numbers dwindling? You should've seen the last soul I reaped. Wore sin like a second skin. I'm doing you a favor, really sparing your precious realms from the filth that would ruin them."

Sol dark gaze sharpened. "And what about Aurora? Is she 'filth' too?"

Malik's grin faltered, and for a split second, his mask cracked. **Damn it.** He saw the god's raised eyebrow and clenched his jaw. **Get it together.**

"Of course she is," he said, but his voice was tighter than it should have been. His hand brushed over his chest as if to ease the ache that formed there every time, he spoke of her this way. "What else would she be?"

Sol's eyes gleamed with something close to pity. "She is far more than that, demon. She's falling in love with you a creature so vile, even the lowest planes would turn you away."

Malik swallowed the bitter taste rising in his throat. "It's just one girl. One soul. Why are you so bothered by it?"

"Because she's no ordinary soul, you fool. She's a dormant goddess."

The words hit Malik like a physical blow.... a goddess?

His mind raced, reeling with the revelation. Aurora? A goddess?

He had known something was different about her, something beyond her beauty, beyond her spirit. She carried a power inside her, but he had assumed it was just another tortured soul, one more human wrestling with pain and despair.

But this—this was something else entirely.

Goddesses weren't like the angels or demons that filled the usual ranks. They were rare, primordial beings, capable of both creation and destruction. Most of them never awakened to their full potential. But if Aurora was one of them…

It explained everything. The hardship she'd endured and the trials she faced in this life were designed to keep her unknowing, unawaken until she could truly ascend. He had thought he was dealing with just another mortal, but she was something infinitely more powerful.

Malik's gut twisted if she awakened everything could change.

Sol's voice broke through his thoughts. "She's been sent to live through this trial unaware of what she is, her divine potential hidden. But now that you've entered her life now that you've begun to corrupt her path could change. If you claim her, you sabotage her destiny."

Malik tried to smirk, but it felt hollow. He had known Aurora was special, but a goddess? "So what? If she's dormant, she doesn't know what she is. Why should it matter to me?"

"Because if you take her now, she will never ascend. She'll be yours forever. But you will have robbed her of everything she could have been."

A cold chill ran through his spine. He'd spent centuries claiming souls, manipulating mortals, and bending them to his will. It had always been just business. But this? This was different. This was her.

And for the first time, the weight of what he was about to do pressed down on him.

If he didn't take her, she might awaken—might ascend to the kind of power that could reshape worlds. But if he claimed her, as he was bound to do, she would never know what she was meant to become. She would belong to him, locked in this mortal coil, forever blind to her true nature.

His heart clenched, the familiar dread settling in his chest. He had been playing with her life with her soul, and now, he realized, with something far greater than he ever understood.

"What happens now?" he asked, his voice quiet, almost a whisper.

Sol smiled grimly. "That's up to you, demon."

If she ascended to the ranks, she would be like the one sitting across from him now his mortal enemy, locked in an eternal struggle, both of them pawn in this endless cosmic game.

He couldn't let that happen, but...

She would be magnificent with her powers fully awakened. The thought filled him with something he hadn't felt in centuries—pain. The idea of her rising above him, so beautiful in her divinity, hurt in ways he didn't fully understand. Another ache throbbed in the heart he hadn't known he possessed until he met her.

Helios, the god sitting opposite him waiting for his response to that bombshell. Keeping his expression neutral or at least hoping he did, Malik gave a mocking smile. "Ah, so it all becomes clear. Well, don't get your feathers in a ruffle. She's my sweet, delicious little prize too. We'll take good care of her where she's going."

"I wonder if telling him that was your wisest decision," Minos remarked, sounding almost like he was scolding the god.

"Yes, I know. He'll be more determined now," Helios muttered, his eyes fixed on Malik with growing intensity.

"I told you from the beginning how determined I was," Malik shot back. "I told you there'd be no changing my mind. Whatever yoke you plan to strap on her in her afterlife makes no difference to me. She's signed over to me, and I intend to take her."

Minos turned to face him, unflinching. "Auroras goddess hood aside, I find the implications of your contract disturbing. If it's honored, it might set a precedent that could have disastrous consequences."

Malik sniffed, forcing a nonchalant tone. "How's that?"

"If word spreads that any mortal can sell another soul for personal gain, especially someone with divine potential, it could create chaos."

Malik leaned forward, his voice cold. "Not any mortal. I didn't pull someone off the street. Andreas was her father, he had a claim to her, and he chose to relinquish it because he's a filthy bastard."

"He's not the only one," Helios muttered darkly.

Minos remained calm. "Regardless, we frown upon these arrangements."

Malik's fingers twitched. He had been toying with the idea of releasing Aurora, but he wanted it to be his decision. If he was going to suffer for losing a soul, it had to be on his terms. Not because he'd been defeated. "Frown all you want. You aren't taking this away from me."

"Helios and I have discussed this at length." So, the god's name was Helios. "We've found ourselves in a gray area, but we've reached a compromise we hope you'll be amenable to. If not, as the holder of the contract, you can refuse. But with a potential goddess at stake, Helios is prepared to take this matter to the Caliphate, and I must say I would be happy to refer it on."

Son of a bitch. The Caliphate, the so-called neutral council, rarely ended well for his kind. If they got involved, it would be a disaster.

"This isn't right," Mailk snapped. "If she weren't a sleeping goddess, you wouldn't even blink. What gives her more value than any other soul? The fact that you want to see her rise with divine power, to strut around as some all-knowing being? That's ridiculous."

Helios's eyes gleamed. "Do you want to hear the terms of our compromise or not?"

Malik's teeth clenched. "Fine. State the terms."

Minos nodded. "It's quite simple. Offer her the same bargain."

"What?" he raised an eyebrow, suspicious.

Helios's voice was smooth. "Her final trial. Make her aware of what's at stake tell her everything. Then give her the option: she can name another to take her place in Hell."

"This is absurd."

Helios pressed on. "If she names another, your contract is fulfilled, and she becomes yours. But you can only take her, not the one she names."

"And if she doesn't name anyone?"

"Then your contract is null and void. You'll destroy it. She'll be completely free from you. She'll awaken to her true potential, and she'll belong to us."

Malik felt a twisted grin tug at his lips. **Diabolical.** If Aurora took the way out, she'd doom herself. He could see her panicking, trying to save herself, only too late to realize what she had done. "Impressive. It's a trap we rarely employ."

The god scoffed. "I doubt that. But it's the only compromise we could offer that you might agree to."

Mailk's eyes narrowed. "I'm surprised you'd go along with this. You're not pressing to get her released without putting her through this torment."

"Don't tempt me."

"Oh, but you're that certain of victory, aren't you? So sure, she's so selfless that she'll never take the deal?"

"If she's truly fit for her divine ascension, and I believe she is, then yes. She will be selfless."

"And if she's not? Well, I suppose you'll have your answer then." Malik chuckled, leaning back. "Either way, I'll enjoy watching her make that choice."

Helios's face hardened. "Are you in agreement or not, demon? I have more important matters than playing games with you."

A vision of Aurora flashed in Malik's mind, her blue eyes filled with trust, her laughter, the way she whispered his name in the dark. The thought of telling her everything of showing her what he truly was, what he had done twisted his insides. Somehow, it seemed worse than just taking her soul in ignorance. He'd have to watch her horror, her pain as she realized who he was.

He wanted to tear the room apart and unleash his rage. If only he had taken her in the parking garage that night. He could have spared himself this torment. If he had claimed her before she had wormed her way into his heart...

He wouldn't have to care.

"Do we have an accord?" Helios's voice cut through the storm of thoughts.

Malik felt cornered, forced into a decision that could cost him everything. Part of him screamed to reject the compromise, to take her soul as planned, no matter the consequences. But the party that had begun to care about her deeply told him to give her a chance.

Dammit. **She'd beaten him.**

All his rage came to a halt, and he stopped pacing, his decision made. For besting him without even knowing it she deserved a chance to escape.

"Fine," he growled. "I'll give her the option. We'll see how it goes."

Out of the corner of his eye, he saw Helios and Minos exchange looks, their heads lifting slightly. But Malik couldn't bear to look at them.

"I'll tell her everything," he said quietly. "We'll see if she chooses."

Minos returned to scribbling in his ledgers, dismissing him. Helios rose, moving toward Malik with a swift, almost silent grace. Malik stiffened, cutting him a sharp glance.

"Don't thank me," Mailk snapped, "or I'll throw you across the room."

Helios smirked. "I was only going to thank you for being reasonable."

"That's almost worse," he sneered. "Coming from someone whose dirty work I'm doing."

The god chuckled, but the smug triumph had faded from his face, replaced by a weariness. "You demons are good for the occasional chuckle, I'll give you that."

Malik's lip curled. He stepped closer to Helios, close enough to feel the other's presence, his voice low and dangerous. "One word of warning before you congratulate yourself. I can be… very convincing. I know terrors she can't even imagine, and I'll make her believe in every single one of them. By the time I'm done, she'll damn every soul she knows to Hell to save herself.

Helios's expression darkened. "We'll see."

Malik felt the grim satisfaction return as he watched the confidence slip from the god's face. It wasn't over yet... not by a long shot.

"Then I suppose it's as you said," Hel muttered, turning away. "We'll see how it goes."

Chapter 12

Tonight was the night. Aurora knew Malik was leaving tomorrow, and the future had been gnawing at her mind. She had waited, hoping he would say something about where things were heading, but he hadn't. Still, she could feel it—every time he held her, kissed her, made love to her. He wanted her there was no mistaking the passion between them. She had never felt this way with anyone else.

They had to talk about it tonight. If he didn't bring it up, she would. She had to be brave. She would tell him she wanted to see him again, that she didn't care how they made it work. He could come to her, or she would go to him anything to avoid the empty bed and aching heart that threatened her now. Aurora knew she was putting herself out there again, and Renee had been right: this could end in disaster. But wasn't that the point? To find the one person who made everything feel different?

If he said that seeing her again wasn't what he wanted… No, she couldn't think about that. The idea of him walking out of her life after tonight was unbearable. Her nights were more peaceful with him next to her as if he could somehow keep the nightmares away. She didn't need promises of forever, but she needed more of him.

Her heart leaped at the knock on the door. Taking a deep breath, she glanced at the dining table one last time. It wasn't much, but the candlelight was soft, and the silverware gleamed. She hoped Malik liked baked ziti it was the only thing she knew how to make well.

She smoothed her dress, twirled toward the living room, and gave herself a quick once-over in the mirror before opening the door. And there he was.

Somehow, he was more beautiful every time she saw him. That smile the way his eyes softened when they met hers made her heart race. Unable to help herself, she stepped into his arms.

But something was wrong.

He didn't pull her close like he usually did like he wanted to meld them into one. His embrace was stiff and distant, and her heart sank. Oh no. Please, don't let this go bad.

Quickly, she stepped back, forcing a smile. "I'm glad you're here. Come on in, food's ready."

He followed her inside silently, closing the door behind him. She tried to keep up the conversation, heading toward the kitchen. "It's just baked ziti. I hope that's okay," she said, the lightness in her voice forced. So much of their time together had been about physical connection, she realized now as her stomach twisted. They hadn't talked much about things like likes, dislikes, or... the future.

Why hadn't they talked about the future?

Suddenly, a thought struck her, stopping her dead in her tracks. How could I be so blind? Aurora gripped the edge of the kitchen island, her knuckles white. All this time, she'd never asked the obvious question. What if...

Her voice wavered as she turned to face him, still holding onto the counter for support. She tried to steady herself, but the words slipped out before she could stop them. "Are you married?"

His brow furrowed, and a flicker of confusion crossed his face. He took too long to respond, his eyes studying her in that unsettling, penetrating way that always made the hair at her nape stand on end. Aurora's mouth moved faster than her mind, filling the silence.

"I can't believe I never asked. I'm such an idiot. If you're here, and you've got a wife at home oh God, if you've got kids, I'm just... I'm just going to…" She felt her breath quicken. "Oh God, I'm going to hell."

He laughed, but the sound was tight, almost pained. "Well, Aurora, I've got good news and bad news. It's up to you which you want to hear first."

Her heart hammered in her chest, her pulse roaring in her ears. "I'll take the good news first."

"I'm not married."

She sagged in relief, one hand going to her heart. "Thank God. You scared the crap out of me don't do that." Whatever the bad news was at least she hadn't been someone's mistress. Once she caught her breath, she looked up at him, the distance between them feeling heavier than ever. "So... the bad news is that this isn't going to work for you, right?"

She could feel the truth pressing down on her now. All her hopes, all the emotions she'd kept in check, were crashing through the surface. "I know you know what I want, Malik. I'd like to see you again. Somehow. But I guess that isn't going to happen, is it?"

"It's not… anything like that." He glanced around the room, gesturing vaguely as if the weight of the entire situation could be summed up with a single motion. "This—" he said, sweeping his hand to encompass her, her apartment, everything between them, "—would work very well for me. More than I'd like to admit."

Her heart jumped with a flicker of hope. "Oh. Well, then… what's the bad news?"

His gaze darkened, and when he spoke, his voice was low. "I'm afraid the bad news is… there's a possibility that you could very well be going to hell."

She stared at him, her mind struggling to process his words. "What?"

His expression was calm but laced with something unreadable, as though he were trying to detach from the moment. "I'm not exactly who you think I am. I've been keeping something from you a lot of things."

Her stomach twisted. **What is he saying?**

"What do you mean, going to hell'? Is that some kind of joke?"

His jaw tightened. "I wish it were." He ran a hand through his dark hair, and for a brief moment, she saw something raw in his eyes, something like regret. "There's more to me than what you see, Aurora and there's more to you, too. You've been marked, and I'm... connected to that."

Marked? Her mind spun. This wasn't real. **It couldn't be real.** "Malik, what are you talking about?"

"I've tried to avoid this conversation. I've tried to... keep you in the dark. But I can't anymore. I came into your life for a reason, and that reason... well, it's not something you'd ever want to hear."

Her legs weakened beneath her, and she leaned against the counter for support. "What are you saying? What the hell are you saying?"

He stepped closer, his voice soft but firm. "I'm not like you, Aurora I'm not human."

The air in the room felt heavy, suffocating. **Not human?** Her breath hitched as the full weight of his words slammed into her. "Then what are you?"

His eyes locked onto hers, and for the first time, she saw the depth of something far darker than she'd ever imagined behind them. "I'm the one who's supposed to take your soul."

Chapter 13

Malik's voice cracked at the end, something he never thought possible not in all the eons he had spent contracting, reaping, and condemning souls. This wasn't supposed to be hard, he was supposed to tear souls from bodies without remorse, without hesitation. But everything had changed when he touched Aurora's soft skin. Since then, he felt like his skin had been turned inside out. Nothing felt natural anymore.

She stared at him, still not fully grasping the weight of what he was trying to say. Confusion clouded her expression. "What are you talking about? Did I do something wrong?"

"No," he said, his voice raw. "You didn't do a thing. It's me. It's always been me." He turned away, unable to meet her eyes. Her father should have died. Andreas had made his deal and upheld his part of the bargain. The man wasn't worth saving, but Aurora... she never deserved any of this.

"I don't understand. What's your fault?" Her voice trembled, unsteady. "Look, if you're trying to end things with me, at least give me a better reason than some vague 'it's not you, it's me' crap."

"I don't want to end things," he said turning to face her. "The problem is, I wanted to be with you forever and can't not without a cost one I don't think you're willing to pay."

She stared at him, clearly bewildered. "You're not making sense."

"I'm not who you think I am, Aurora," he admitted, his voice hoarse. "I'm not even what you think I am. The night you saw me wasn't the first time. I've been watching you your entire life not just this one all of them."

Her eyes widened, and she took a step back. "What are you saying? That's not possible."

He exhaled deeply. "I've been following you all your lives, and in this one, I made a deal with your father. He traded your soul for his life and now you belong to me."

Her face drained of color. Good, he thought maybe now she'd believe it.

"My father? I don't even know my father," she whispered.

"You didn't need to know him for him to make the deal. His name was Andreas."

She gasped, her eyes widening in disbelief. He saw her begin to piece things together, her face paling as fear finally took hold.

"You need to leave," she said, her voice trembling.

"I can't," he said softly. "Not until I get your answer."

Her eyes welled with tears. "I can't do this. I can't do this to someone else, and I can't do this to myself either. I hate you for this."

I hate me too.

He took a step forward, but she recoiled, stumbling back. "Please, just go."

He stood still, the weight of her words pressing down on him. "Whether you feel you can or not, you must decide, Aurora."

"Decide what?" she shouted, her voice rising. "You want me to damn someone else so you can take me to Hell instead? That's not a choice. That's a death sentence!"

Her anger erupted then, pure and raw. "I don't belong to you. I don't belong to anyone!" Her voice cracked with emotion, and she screamed, "I didn't ask for this!"

She reached for the nearest object, a picture frame, and hurled it at him. It shattered against the wall. Then, her eyes locked on the cross hanging nearby. She grabbed it and held it to her chest, her expression triumphant.

"That won't help you," he said quietly. "Not against me."

She threw it at him anyway, and he dodged it easily. When he looked back, she had crumpled against the wall, sinking to the floor her sobs were muffled by the carpet every one of them stabbed him like a knife to the chest.

He couldn't stand it anymore. The need to reach out, to comfort her, overwhelmed him but she would reject him. She would scream, fight, and maybe even hurt herself. What could he do?

Quietly, he knelt beside her, careful not to startle her further. The urge to touch her was overwhelming, but he fought it down.

"Aurora," he whispered. "I'll leave. I'm not going to lay a hand on you. You don't have to answer now. I need you to understand I didn't want this. I didn't want to scare you. I'll do everything I can to fix this, I swear." His voice broke. "Just… don't be afraid of me when I come back."

Her sobs quieted. Slowly, she lifted her head, her eyes swollen and red. "What if you can't fix it?" she asked in a broken voice. "Are you going to take me? Can't you just let me go?"

Her pleading eyes, her shattered voice they nearly undid him. He wanted to rip the contract to pieces and damn the consequences. But he couldn't. Not yet.

"I don't know," he admitted. His gaze lingered on her for a moment longer before he stood. He strode toward the door, fighting the urge to tear it from its hinges in his fury. He needed to leave and needed to breathe. The air in her apartment was suffocating, and the sight of her breaking apart was more than he could bear.

Slamming the door behind him, he stepped into the cool night air, but it brought no relief. None of this would matter. He could spend centuries in Hell, punishing himself, and he would still be no closer to a solution for her. **He'd fucked up.** That was the truth of it. He'd fucked up, and he'd fallen in love with her.

He stopped in the parking lot, his chest heaving with frustration. His shields were still raised, protecting him from prying eyes, but he couldn't contain the rage.

Throwing his head back, he roared to the heavens. "Helios!"

The name echoed through the air, vibrating with fury and desperation.

He would get answers one way or another.

***

Aurora stared at her closed front door, numb and trembling. The weight of everything that had just happened was crushing her. How had her life come to this? She wanted nothing more than to crawl into bed and never get up again, never have to face the world or anyone in it.

I've gone from dating guys who ghost me to dating guys who want to kill me. She shuddered at the thought, hating what her life had become. What's next?

These dark, sarcastic thoughts were keeping her sane because the truth was too much to bear. Malik is evil, the words echoed in her mind, impossible to shake. She had always felt a little off about him, but she'd never expected **this**.

Wiping her tear-streaked face, she forced herself to stand. Get up. Deal with it. It was what she always did even when she felt like she couldn't. Her legs wobbled beneath her as she made her way to the door and locked it, her fingers trembling. She couldn't afford to fall apart now. Not yet.

In the bathroom, she splashed cold water on her face, the shock of it jolting her awake to a world she didn't want to be in anymore. Staring at her reflection in the mirror, she barely recognized herself. Pale skin, hollow eyes she looked haunted. Even her lips were thin and compressed as if holding back the sobs threatening to break free. Her hair was a mess from wallowing on the floor, tangling in Malik's shirt as she'd cried.

A fresh wave of tears surged inside her, but she fought them back. **No. Not again.** She stumbled into her bedroom, the sight of her neatly turned-down bed almost breaking her. She had imagined spending the night with him there dreamed of it and now those dreams were shattered, just like every other hope she had held on to.

Had he been planning to kill me all along? The thought hit her like a punch to the gut. Her breath caught, and her legs nearly gave out beneath her. Memories of their time together crashed over her how passionate he'd been, how intense. Was he thinking about dragging me to Hell even then?

Her mind flashed to the mugger that first night, the way he had laid his hand on the man's chest, and the man had screamed and dropped. **Oh God.** And then she remembered how, that same night, he had placed his hand over her heart while they were together. The same strange sensation had washed over her, one she hadn't understood at the time. She had pulled his hand away and kissed it, and the feeling had stopped.

Was he going to do it then?

She wrapped her arms around herself, shaking. God, my love life was a disaster before, but this? She remembered Renee's dramatic declaration: *"Men are only good for murdering the soul."* Ha. Well, Renee, I've got one for you.

A small, bitter laugh bubbled up from her throat, it felt almost hysterical like she was teetering on the edge of something too dark to fathom. She couldn't call Renee. There's no one to turn to, no one who would understand. What would she even say? Hey, Ren, guess what? The guy I've been seeing is a demon who's been stalking me through all my lives and now he wants to take me to Hell. Yeah. That wouldn't go over well.

The crushing weight of that thought settled over her like a suffocating blanket. She sank onto the edge of the bed, staring blankly at the wall. There was no one to help her. No one could comprehend what she was going through.

I'm alone in this. Completely, utterly alone.

***

"Helios!" Malik's voice tore through the night, filled with an urgency he never thought he'd associate with calling upon an angel.

If the bastard didn't answer him…

"You called?"

The smooth voice behind him made Malik whirl around. There stood the God arms crossed a quizzical look on his serene face.

"I want out of this," he growled.

Helios's eyebrows shot upward. "What?"

"I said I want out. I want this to... go away."

The God stared at him for a moment, then laughed. A soft, mocking sound. "Trying to keep yourself out of hot water, are you?"

Malik's jaw clenched. "I don't want to overlook an easy solution."

Helios's expression sobered, though the amusement still danced in his eyes. "Sorry, but no. There's no hidden rule to nullify the contract. If you want out, you'll have to break it yourself. Only you."

He cursed under his breath. That had been his fear, but it was worth a shot. "What happens to her if I do? What have I done? Have I... ruined her chances?"

Helios tilted his head, considering the question with a thoughtful hum. "Probably not. I'd need confirmation of course but she can't be held responsible for what you did to her. She's still a goddess."

He pulled the contract from his jacket, the black string that bound it fraying beneath his fingers as he ripped it off. He unfurled the parchment, staring at the words he once thought would give him everything he wanted. Now, they just mocked him.

"You love her," Helios said quietly.

"How astute," Malik snapped.

"Oh, I've known from the start," the God replied. "Ever since I was assigned this case, I wondered why you didn't take her when she came of age. Every time you got close, you pulled back. You gave her more time. It was clear to anyone watching you were in love with her. Even through her many lives."

Malik glared at him. "You and Minos did this on purpose, didn't you? The two-week stay, forcing her into this decision you knew all along I wouldn't follow through."

Helios's smile was infuriatingly cryptic. "Maybe."

Malik's frustration bubbled up, but he bit it back. "I don't care. I want to know that she'll be all right."

"She'll be perfectly fine," he said, his tone softening. "How could she not be? You'll be out of her life."

Out of her life. That stung but it was true. He was the source of her suffering, the dark cloud that had followed her through lifetimes. She'd be better off without him.

"I don't want to be her problem anymore. But... what if something happens to her? What if she needs me, and I'm gone?"

Helios's expression turned wary. "What are you asking?"

He swallowed hard. The words stuck in his throat, but he forced them out. "I need you to promise me something."

Helios frowned, his serene demeanor cracking just slightly. "And that is?"

Malik's fingers tightened around the edges of the parchment. "I've never broken a contract like this. I don't know what's going to happen to me when I do."

"They can't strike at her again," Helios reassured him. "New rules were set after an incident in another case. Once the contract is destroyed, she's free."

Malik nodded, the knot in his chest loosening a little. But the fear of what would happen to Aurora still gnawed at him. "I need more than that. I want her protected."

Helios raised an eyebrow. "I can't personally interfere. She has to make her own choices to earn her memories. You know that."

Mailk's gaze fell to the contract in his hands. "I know. But... can you at least petition for her to be placed under divine protection? Even for a time?"

Helios was silent for a moment, then he gave a nod. "I can do that."

"Thank you."

They stood for a long moment, the tension thick between them. Finally, Helios spoke. "Are you going to do it?"

Malik's hands trembled as he gripped the top of the contract. The realization of what he was about to do hit him like a punch to the gut Lucifer will kill him for this. There was no doubt in his mind anymore destroying this contract was a death sentence for him.

But if he didn't, Aurora would be lost forever and that was a price he couldn't pay.

"You would truly do this for her? Sacrifice yourself?" Helios asked, his voice quiet now, the sarcasm gone.

Malik closed his eyes, and Aurora's face filled his mind. He pictured her smiling beautifully and then he saw her with wings, bathed in an ethereal light, as she was meant to be a goddess.

"With all my heart," he whispered.

With a single motion, he tore the contract in two.

The parchment split cleanly, the edges crackling with a faint glow of magic as the words and sigils dissolved into the air, disappearing into the night. Malik's heart clenched, and a hollow emptiness filled him as the bond between him and Aurora shattered.

Helios stood still, watching him, his expression unreadable. "It's done."

He nodded, but the weight of the act pressed down on him like the world itself had shifted. **It's done.**

He had lost her.

He had saved her.

But he had lost her.

"You know what this means for you," Helios said quietly.

"Yeah," Malik muttered, staring at the torn pieces falling from his hands. "I know."

Helios's gaze softened, just for a moment. "I'll make sure she's protected."

"Good," Malik said, his voice barely audible.

He didn't wait for his response. With one last look at the
pieces dissolving into nothing, he turned and walked
away, disappearing into the shadows.

It was over.

Chapter 14

Aurora lay on her bed, her body trembling and her chest tight as sobs wracked through her. She felt like she couldn't breathe, like something inside her had snapped. Oh God, what's happening to me?

Then, just as suddenly as the attack had come, it was gone. She gasped for air, filling her lungs to their fullest, desperate to keep inhaling as if more air could fill the empty places in her soul. She felt a sense of peace, unlike anything she'd ever known. It washed over her, soothing the jagged edges of fear and sorrow gnawing at her for as long as she could remember.

Was this real? It felt too good to be real.

She exhaled slowly as if letting go of all the bad things she had carried for so long. The more she breathed, the more the dread and fear seemed to seep out of her with every breath. Was she crazy? Maybe, but whatever this was, it felt good.

A soft knock startled her from her thoughts. Malik.

Her heart pounded as she made her way to the living room, her legs still unsteady beneath her. She peeked through the window and saw him standing at her door, his head bowed, his shoulders hunched in a way she'd never seen before. He rubbed a hand over his face, and she hesitated. Should I even let him in?

Whatever had happened, something was different now. She could feel it. Leaving the chain on, she cracked the door open. When his head lifted, she nearly gasped. The devastation on his face and the sorrow in his eyes made her stomach twist.

"What is it?" she asked, her voice trembling.

He gave her a sad smile, but there was no warmth. "I just wanted you to know you're free. All is as it should be."

Her heart stuttered. "They let me go?"

"No," he said quietly. "**I** let you go."

She blinked, her mind racing. "What do you mean? You're just… going to let me go?"

"I hope you get everything out of life that you wish for, Aurora." He turned, about to walk away.

"Wait!" she cried, not knowing what compelled her. She shut the door to unlatch the chain and flung it open. "Where are you going?"

He didn't turn to face her. "Home."

"Oh." Her throat tightened. "You mean…"

"Yes."

"Will I ever see you again?" Her voice was small, almost afraid to ask.

He shook his head slowly as if even saying the words would break him. "No."

Her fingers went to her lips, trembling. She could feel the relief in her soul, the curse was lifted, she could finally breathe, and she was free but there was something more. Something in his face, the way his hands trembled ever so slightly as he shoved them into his pockets, told her he'd given up more than she could ever understand.

He'd sacrificed something for her.

"I can't say I never meant to hurt you," he said, his voice thick. "There was a time when I did. I had fun at your expense but now I realize… I never would have taken you. I couldn't." He paused, then, as if deciding whether he should touch her. Her heart raced as she stared up at him. A moment later, his hand cradled the side of her face, his thumb gently brushing away a tear she hadn't realized had fallen. "I love you."

"Malik…" she whispered, her heart breaking for him.

"If you ever felt the same, even for a moment tell me now. Tell me before I have to go."

Her breath hitched. She nodded. "I did. I loved you."

He swallowed, accepting her words with a faint smile. It was all she could give him, but it was enough. Her hand slid over his, holding it there, unwilling to let go. "I feel… different now like everything's going to be okay."

He nodded, his dark eyes full of something she couldn't read. "It is. For the first time in your life, or at least as long as you can remember, I won't be involved anymore. The curse is lifted you're free."

"But… you did this for me," she whispered, her voice breaking. "You didn't have to."

His eyes darkened, his hand slipping away from her. "Don't make me out to be a hero. I've been nothing but a villain to you."

"Maybe you've spent so long telling yourself that, you can't see anything else," she said softly. "But I've seen the good in you."

"You haven't seen half the evil." His voice was harsh, but there was pain behind it. Despite her grasping fingers he pulled his hand away completely and stepped back. The distance between them felt too wide, her skin tingling from the absence of his touch.

He nodded once, stiffly. "Thank you, Aurora."

"Don't go yet—"

But he was already turning his back to her as he walked away. Her heart clenched as she watched him round the corner, disappearing down the stairs to the parking lot. *Please, look back at me.*

He didn't.

She stood in the doorway, her fingers trembling against the wood. She was free, but a strange emptiness settled in her chest. She didn't want him to go, not like this. But she couldn't move, couldn't run after him. He didn't want her to follow.

And so, she stayed, the door open, as she stared at the space where he had been.

***

Malik had expected them to drag him back, probably thought they'd expect him to run but he was done with cowardice. He'd made his choice. He was going to face whatever was waiting for him.

After rounding the corner of Aurora's building out of sight of her door and stopped. His gaze fell to the ground as he willed the earth to swallow him up. *I've done it. She's free.* But the thought brought little comfort. He wanted to look back, just once, but he knew one look at her, and I'd run back to her. Run straight into her arms and stay there until they force him to leave.

Whatever punishment they had in store for him, it would be a mercy compared to the pain of letting her go. Either they'd take his mind off her, or they'd kill him and right now, he couldn't say which option he preferred.

He felt the power rising around him, dark and oppressive, pulling at his feet. The familiar sensation of magic crept over his legs, into his torso, reaching his arms and fingers. Soon, it would rise to his head, consuming him entirely. Once it does, I'll be gone.

Malik tipped his head back, staring up at the sky. The branches of a nearby tree cut intricate patterns against the glittering stars, and he wished, at that moment, that the sky was blue like her eyes. Her eyes were no longer shadowed by the curse he had placed on her. She belonged up there, in the heavens, beyond the clouds, not where he was going.

He'd done the right thing. I can take comfort in that but even now, as the searing power of Hell's magic rose higher, the thought of her left a hollow ache in his chest.

" Malakiás ."

The voice startled him, and as the power of the underworld slipped over his mouth and nose, never his favorite part, like drowning he glanced over.

Helios stood next to the tree, his serene expression unchanged.

"Good luck to you," the God said softly.

He managed a nod, though he doubted luck had any place where he was headed. Then the magic completed its journey, pulling him under. The ground cracked open beneath him, and he was swallowed whole by a whirlwind of heat and screams, the sickly reddish-orange glow of Hell's fire rising to meet him. **This is my fate.** The only thing he could do now was hope she never knew what he'd sacrificed.

***

"Malik!" Aurora's voice tore from her throat as she sprinted around the corner of the building. She raced through the narrow passage between the apartments and the aging brown fence, her breath catching in her chest. She had expected to find him still walking along the grassy path, but the only thing that greeted her was the wind and the rustling of a lone tree's limbs.

She slowed, her heart sinking. The wind carried an acrid scent of sulfur, it stung her nostrils. He's gone.

She pulled her sweater tighter around her, a chill creeping over her that had nothing to do with the weather. **Why did I come?** She hadn't thought it through. She didn't even know what she wanted to say when she found him but the way things had ended between them at the door hadn't felt right. There was unfinished business.

He gave me my life back. No, that wasn't accurate. Because of him, I never had much of a life yet none of that mattered now. She needed to see him speak to him to make him understand what she couldn't find the words for before.

"Malik!" she shouted again, her voice swallowed by the wind. She started to run again, heading toward the courtyard, hoping against hope that maybe he hadn't left yet. But the further she went, the more certain she became that he was already gone.

Her heart clenched. **No.** It couldn't end like this. She had so many questions, so many things left unsaid.

A broken sob ripped from her throat. "No."

Tears slipped down her face as she slowed her pace, the emptiness of the courtyard mocking her. She had lost him, just like that, and now she'd never get the answers she needed. She turned, wiping her cheeks, and began the slow trudge back to her apartment, her steps heavy with regret.

Then, something hit her.

Not something... a force.

She was wrenched sideways with such force that it knocked the air from her lungs. Her back slammed hard against the wooden fence, pain blooming in her chest as the world spun around her. Before she could process what was happening, a hand gripped her throat, squeezing with bone-crushing strength.

Her wide eyes met the hateful, glowing red gaze of a man she'd never seen before. His face twisted with fury, his orange hair wild around his head, and his other hand pressed against her chest. Pain exploded inside her, a burning agony that reached deeper than anything physical. Her very soul felt like it was being ripped from her body.

She tried to scream for Malik, but no sound came out. *Malik, help me!*

The darkness closed in fast. She could no longer see, barely feel. Just as she thought everything was slipping away, she heard something—a flutter, like the beat of a thousand wings. Then, an enraged shout, followed by an answering roar. The air around her crackled with energy, and the sounds of a vicious fight erupted nearby.

She was too weak, too numb to move. All she could do was lie there, her body useless, listening as the battle raged on.

"You can't touch her soul. It is written!" one of the voices snarled, a clear, piercing tone that cut through the chaos.

"I can still kill the whore," the other voice growled back, low and menacing.

"Kill her, and she goes with me. You've still lost."

Her mind struggled to make sense of the words, but everything felt distant and foggy. Was she dead? She couldn't feel the ground beneath her or the cold grass that should have been pressing against her cheek.

She couldn't move, couldn't speak.

The only thing she could do was listen to the clashing voices above her, a strange mix of supernatural energy and rage. One voice, sharp and crystalline, pierced through the darkness. The other, deep and demonic, sent shivers down her spine. Neither of them was Malik.

But where was he? *Malik, please… I need you.*

The fighting reached a crescendo, the sounds of blows landing and grunts of pain filling the air. Aurora wanted to get up, to run and flee from this nightmare but her body refused to respond.

Paralyzed. Whatever he did to you, you're paralyzed. The thought whispered through her mind, terrifying her more than the pain had.

Oh God, help me…

And then, silence. Absolute, terrifying silence. Am I deaf now, too? But no—a voice clear and cutting like glass, broke through the void.

"Aurora?"

Her heart stuttered. She wanted to answer, but no words would come. Would he think she was dead if she couldn't respond?

The voice sighed, closer now, filled with regret. "Oh, Aurora. I should have seen this coming."

Seen what coming? She wanted to scream, to demand answers, but her lips wouldn't move. Tears welled behind her closed eyes. *Malik, where are you?*

The frustration was unbearable. She wanted to cry, to fight, to get away from whatever was happening, but all she could do was lie there, helpless, as the unknown figure loomed over her.

Chapter 15

Helios stared down at the crumpled figure of Aurora on the ground and felt a surge of anger he hadn't experienced in centuries. He wanted to tear through every realm, drag every demon involved into the Underworld, and make them answer for this, especially the one responsible for her suffering: Malik.

But his anger was short-lived. He'd lied to Malik, assuring him that everything would be fine, and now, looking at Aurora's limp form, he cursed himself. He had overestimated the demon's willingness to follow the ancient rules. *I've been a fool.*

Kimaris, the cowardly demon who relished chaos and violence, had attacked her and retreated to his dark domain, leaving Helios to clean up the mess. Her soul was hanging on by a thread, a shimmering overlay of her body, flickering in and out of this world. Another moment and she'd have been gone completely. He would have been forced to take her to the realms beyond.

What choice do I have now? He couldn't restore her, not in the state she was in, but neither could he leave her like this, half in and half out of life.

Helios knelt beside her and called his fellow gods, knowing they would hear him. "This is Helios, requesting immediate aid for transport of a mortal woman. Coordinates follow."

A few moments later, a voice came through his mind. "This is Aceso. I'm on my way, I'll be there in ten minutes."

He nodded to himself. Aceso would know what to do. If Aurora were taken to a mortal hospital, they wouldn't understand what had happened to her and gods rarely intervened directly in mortal affairs... this was already a breach.

Kneeling next to her, he placed a hand on her head, feeling the turmoil in her mind. Her thoughts were tangled with fear, pain, and confusion. She was slipping away.

"Aurora, can you hear me?" he asked gently, using his connection to reach her. "You don't have to speak. Just think your response."

Her mental voice was faint, trembling. "What happened to me?"

"Malik told you who he was, didn't he?" he replied, his tone soft.

"Yes..."

"That was one of his superiors who attacked you he didn't succeed in killing you, but now... you're in between."

"In between?" Her confusion grew. "Where is Malik? I need him."

"I'm sorry, Aurora. I will try to help you." He wished he had better answers for her, but her situation was delicate, and nothing was certain.

"Who are you?" she asked, her thoughts fragmented.

"My name is Helios, I'm a god."

"You're… like Malik?"

"No," he said, his voice steady. "I'm not like him. I serve a different purpose."

Worry flooded her thoughts, and he could feel her struggle to comprehend. She was starting to piece together the implications of what had happened why she was speaking to a god, and why this was happening to her.

"Can I be saved?" she asked, her voice laced with fear.

"That depends on what you mean by salvation," he answered honestly.

"I want to go back to how I was before…"

He sighed, his heart heavy. *I don't have the answers she needs.* "Just rest for now, Aurora. Someone is coming to take care of you. Aceso is like me but bound to the mortal realm. You won't be able to communicate with her the way you can with me, but she'll keep you safe."

Her fear spiked again. "But where are you going?"

"I have to see what can be done to fix this. I'll stay with you until she arrives just hold on."

She fell silent, left with no choice but to trust him. He knew she was still thinking about Malik. Her thoughts, broken and scattered, always returned to him. She wanted to know where he was, if he was all right if he would come back for her.

He couldn't bring himself to tell her the truth that he didn't know.

A few minutes later, headlights swept over the fence beside them, and he looked up to see a black SUV pull up. The passenger door opened, and Aceso stepped out, hurrying toward them. She was dressed all in black, her blonde hair tied back, her eyes narrowing as she took in the sight of Aurora.

"Oh no," she whispered.

Helios nodded grimly. "Thank you for coming so quickly."

"What happened?" she asked, kneeling beside Aurora, her hands brushing the glowing outline of the young woman's soul.

"She was attacked by Kimaris," he replied.

Acceso's expression darkened. "Helios, you should have let him finish at least she wouldn't be suffering like this."

"I know," he muttered. But it still felt wrong. She had just been given her life back, and now it was hanging in the balance once more.

Before Aceso could reply, another voice joined them. "Kimaris's stench lingers."

Helios turned to see Alvaden, Aceso's lover, striding toward them. He bent down, effortlessly lifting Aurora into his arms, cradling her limp form as if she weighed nothing.

"We can discuss this later," Alvaden said sharply. "For now, we need to get her out of here."

Helios blinked, surprised to see him here. Once a demon of destruction himself, Alavden had been bound to the mortal realm, no longer a force of chaos. But it was still jarring to see him so close to matters of divine intervention.

"I wasn't expecting you," Helios said.

Alvaden's lips twisted into a smirk. "I live for excitement in this dreary mortal existence."

Aceso rolled her eyes as she climbed into the driver's seat. "As if you don't find enough trouble on your own."

"Only when I'm with you, my love," he replied with a grin.

"Take care of her," Helios said, his voice steady, though he still felt unsure. He had to trust Alvaden, even if his past made it difficult.

"I will," he replied, his voice more serious now as he looked down at Aurora's pale face. "I know who she is."

"Of course you do," Helios said bitterly. "She's been a target for your kind for ages."

Alvaden's eyes flashed with anger. "Not *my* kind anymore. I've left that life behind."

Helios held his gaze, acknowledging the truth. Alvaden wasn't bound to the chaos demons anymore, but the reminder of his past still lingered in the back of Helios's mind.

"What do you suggest we do?" Helios asked, feeling the weight of the situation pressing down on him.

Alvaden's black eyes gleamed with a dark understanding. "You can't fix this, Helios. Aceso and I can't fix it either but a demon like Malik can."

Helios stared at him, shocked. "What?"

"They can return what's been taken within a reasonable amount of time," Alvaden explained. "Her soul hasn't left, but it's barely hanging on a demon like him can reattach it."

Helios's mind raced. *Malik.* The one who had started all this was the only one who could save her now.

Alvaden smirked. "So, if you want to save her, your mission is clear: find the one demon who can."

Chapter 16

Malik had no idea how long he'd been trapped here in the abyss, bound and tortured. The suffocating blackness of nonexistence would have been a mercy, but instead, he was chained, knowing only too well what had been done to Aurora after his return but with no knowledge of what had become of her.

A familiar, loathsome voice slithered near his ear. "How are we doing today, Malakiás?" the sadistic tormentor sneered. He didn't know who the bastard was, hidden behind the mask that blocked his vision. All he wished for was one moment to get his hands around his tormentor's throat.

Pain erupted from his side, a scaring burn, and his body convulsed against the chains that held him. His limbs strained against the restraints, but he refused to give the satisfaction of a scream. He gritted his teeth so hard he thought they might shatter.

"So stoic, aren't we? I wonder how your little whore is doing? Do you think she would welcome me as sweetly as she did you? I doubt she could even resist—she can't move, she can't fight, she can't even scream." The tormentor laughed, a cruel sound that clawed at Malik's mind.

Malik's rage roared to life, drowning out the physical agony. "You'd better hope I never get out of here, you son of a bitch," he spat, straining at the chains again, ignoring the pain.

The tormentor chuckled darkly, pouring salt into the open wounds. "Get out of here? You're delusional. Imagine how frightened she is, waiting for you to save her but you won't. She'll waste away, and it'll break your heart. And that's what you are now, isn't it? A romantic. A demon with a broken heart." The voice slithered with sadistic glee. "Are there tears in your eyes now, Malik? I'd gouge them out for you, but I'll wait until the suffering becomes unbearable."

Rage and despair tangled in Malik's chest, almost choking him. *Helios.* He clung to the thought of the god who had spared Aurora before. Helios wouldn't let her suffer, wouldn't abandon her. But even if Helios had to let her die, she would be beyond pain. She would find peace.

Malik's thoughts spun, the knowledge of Madeleine's suffering the only thing keeping him sharp. I have to stay sharp. I have to find a way out. He'd survive this, not for himself, but for her.

"Enough," a new voice commanded, cutting through the torture. The pain stopped, leaving Malik hanging from his chains, his weight dragging against the metal cuffs that bit into his wrists. The voice belonged to Ordog.

"Where the hell have you been?" Malik growled. "Too ashamed to face me? You know what you did." He couldn't see Ordog behind the mask, but he didn't need sight to feel the arrogance dripping from the other demon.

"I follow orders, Malik," he said coolly. "Just like you were supposed to. I'm not here because of anything I've done. You're here because of your own choices."

"Fuck you. You don't know what I've been through."

Ordog gave a short, humorless laugh. "What you've been through? You spent the last two weeks wrapped up in that woman's bed. You let the God outmaneuver you. You had time, but you squandered it. You allowed yourself to get attached. You failed, Malik. You let Helios, and worse, your own heart, make a fool of you and us."

"I don't give a damn how foolish I look. Not anymore." Malik's voice was a snarl but lacked the fire it once held. *I failed Aurora.*

Ordog sighed, though the sound was far from sympathetic. "You were once great, Malik. Now look at you."

Great? He laughed bitterly. He'd been powerful, terrifying, maybe even worshipped at times, but greatness? *No.* His only glimpse of greatness had been in her arms, where he'd found something far more precious than power. Tearing up that contract had been his one act of greatness, and it cost him everything.

"Ordog," he tried, his voice softer now "we were allies once. Friends. If you ever cared for me, release me. Let me help her. She's not ours anymore. What does it matter to you if she lives?"

The moment he said it, he knew it was the wrong thing to ask. Ordog's voice turned cold, venomous. "It matters to me because it torments you. Knowing she's suffering, knowing she may die, beyond your reach forever will break you. Once she's gone, I might even recommend your release. Perhaps you'll rebuild yourself, the creature you were before she tore you apart."

Malik's stomach twisted, his rage turning into a cold, simmering fury. *Release me, and we'll see what happens.* He swallowed the bile rising in his throat. *Play the part. Survive.* "You're right," he lied smoothly. "I should've acted sooner. I'll accept my punishment. Just let me go when… when the time comes."

Ordog paused, considering. "We'll see about that. It's possible, not guaranteed."

Malik heard Ordog's footsteps retreating, but his relief was short-lived. His tormentor stepped forward again, chuckling darkly.

"Miss me?" the voice hissed.

Malik forced a grin, laughing defiantly. "Like I miss your mother," he shot back. They wouldn't break him—not as easily as they thought.

"Laugh while you can, Malik I'm going to carve my name into your chest."

"Make sure you spell it right," He spat, setting his teeth, bracing himself for the inevitable pain. *This isn't over.* Not by a long shot. *Aurora, hold on.*

Time was a blur in the dungeon. Days could feel like mere moments or stretch into eternity. Malik's sense of it was utterly lost. All he knew was that every second spent here was one less second, he had to help Aurora. His desperation simmered, growing cold and bitter.

"How long have I been here?" he rasped, his voice weak, his body sagging against the cursed chains that bound him.

A cruel laugh came in response. "What makes you think I'd tell you that?" Metal scraped against metal, grating on his already raw nerves. The sound echoed in the dark space, each note a reminder of his helplessness. *What now?* he wondered, the scraping sound raising a new wave of dread.

He couldn't see anything with the mask strapped to his face, but maybe that was a blessing. Whatever the demon was preparing to do, Malik knew it would be bad. *Maybe I'm better off not seeing it.* His magic, the force that made him formidable, had long since been stripped away. His once powerful form had fallen apart, his wings tattered, his body encrusted in dried blood, his claws blunted from constant struggle. If she could see him now, she'd scream and run.

The thought of her gave him a sudden surge of fury, a desperate energy that hadn't been there before. He roared and jerked against the chains the sound echoing throughout the dungeon. *Aurora… I'm losing her.*

"Well, well," the tormentor hissed. "Showing some fight again, are we? Good. I enjoy breaking that spirit."

Malik heard the sound of shuffling feet and hands working at the chains. He tensed, ready to fight, to escape if he could, but he was too weak. When they finally released him, he crumpled to the ground like a rag doll. Laughter echoed above him as they lifted him and strapped him to another device.

He wouldn't beg. No matter what they did, he wouldn't give them that satisfaction. But inwardly, he prayed to anyone who could hear him. *Aurora, hold on. Please.*

"Stop!" A voice cut through the din, and Malik almost didn't believe it.

Helios? No, it couldn't be. That voice had never been welcome before, but now it felt like salvation itself.

The other demons hissed, recoiling at the presence of something pure and divine in their dark lair. Helios, with his shining golden robes, must have looked like a glaring beacon in the squalor of the dungeon. *Holy fuck, it really is him.*

"I have an order from The Caliphate," Helios announced, his voice calm and authoritative. "He is to be released at once."

Ordog's cold voice echoed from the entrance, cutting through the tension. "Release him but know this isn't over, god."

"It is for now," Helios countered, walking closer. "Now get him out of this cursed contraption."

A moment later, Malik felt hands undoing his restraints, freeing him from the device. His arms fell limp, and when the heavy mask was finally unlocked and pulled from his head, he groaned in relief. The blinding light of Helios's presence forced his eyes shut again, his body far too weak to handle the brilliance of the god.

When he finally cracked his eyes open, he was met with the glowing protective amulet hanging around Helios's neck, the only thing keeping the god safe in this wretched place.

"Thank you," Malik whispered, his voice hoarse. He could barely stand, his weight fully supported by Helios's strong arms.

Helios's face was all business, but there was a flicker of urgency in his eyes. "Aurora needs your help are you willing to accept mine to get to her?"

"With everything that's in me," he croaked. He'd do anything to save her.

Ordog's voice cut through the moment, sharp as a blade. "If you leave here to help her, you die, Malakiás I'm done with this game. You'll face the slowest, most agonizing death imaginable."

Helios ignored him. "And you will help her?" he asked again, his voice steady, but there was something heavy in the way he asked the question.

"You even have to ask?" he gasped, struggling to maintain his footing as Helios supported him.

"Yes, I do," Helios said. His gaze was piercing, demanding the truth.

"I would do anything for her," Malik said, his voice broken but full of conviction. "I'd let you put me back on that rack if it meant saving her."

Helios gave a single nod. "Good but there is one more thing I need from you before we do this."

"Anything," he whispered. *Whatever it takes.*

As Helios started leading him toward the entrance, supporting him step by step, he muttered, "Don't let her see you like this. By the gods, you're ugly."

Malik let out a weak laugh, grateful for the brief flicker of humor.

Chapter 17

Aurora lay in the dark void, the days blending into an endless stretch of nothingness. Since Helios had left, she had no concept of time and how long she had been like this. It could have been days, maybe more. Aceso had assured her that she was safe and that she was resting in a bed. At least I'm comfortable, she thought, though it was hard to feel comfort when her body felt completely detached from the world.

Aceso had been her lifeline, speaking to her to keep her company even when she couldn't respond. She had talked to Aurora, read to her, and given her glimpses into her life. There were occasional conversations with a man named Alvaden, Aceso's lover, judging by the way they flirted. *They're in love.* Aurora wondered if she and Malik could ever have that if she could be free to love him.

Her thoughts drifted, swirling in the blackness. So much had happened so quickly, turning her world upside down. One day, Malik had been a mysterious man who intrigued her; the next, he was a demon bound to take her soul. Yet, somehow, she still wanted him—loved him. *How ridiculous is that?*

But then her thoughts shifted to the future. *Would she even have one?* The curse on her had been lifted, and for the first time in her life, she wanted to live. Really live, to experience the world in a way she had never before, free from the nightmares that had plagued her.

Her heart ached at the thought of missing out on that chance.

Suddenly, the silence was shattered by noise outside the room. There were shouts, and fear rushed through her. *Is it happening again?* She'd been terrified that someone would come back to finish the job, but Aceso reassured her that she was protected.

The door banged open, and her panic flared. **No, no…**

"Aurora!" Aceso's voice was high with excitement, not fear. "Helios's back! He's brought Malik!"

"Aurora," came Malik's deep voice, familiar yet raw with emotion. *His voice,* the one she had longed to hear since this nightmare began, was like a balm to her soul. But he didn't sound right. Something about him was off. She mentally reached out, desperate for answers.

"Helios!" she called in her mind. "Is he okay?"

"He's fine," he answered gently. "Weakened, but he's here, and he's okay."

"Please tell him to hold my hand," she begged. *If she couldn't feel anything, at least she could know he was there, touching her.*

"He already is, sweetheart," Helios's voice soothed. "Like he's never going to let go again."

"I love him," she whispered through the mental connection, wanting Malik to know before it was too late.

"You can tell him yourself in a moment," he replied softly.

Malik's breath was warm against her ear as he whispered, "I'm here, Aurora. It's going to be all right. I'm going to fix this."

Her heart swelled with hope, the despair she had been battling falling away. *He'll fix it. He always said he would.* Despite everything, she trusted him, maybe more than she should, but there was no denying it. Whatever had happened between them before, it no longer mattered. All she wanted was him; if he felt the same, she was ready to face whatever came next.

He squeezed her hand, and to her shock, she squeezed back. *I felt that.* For the first time since this nightmare began, she could feel something. Her excitement surged, her muscles jerking to life.

"Easy," he soothed. "Just relax. Let it work."

His hand was warm against her chest like the night he'd touched her for the first time but now, instead of pulling her life away, he was returning it. She felt warmth seeping from his palm into her body, spreading through her limbs like fire. The sensation came flooding back in waves, almost too intense to bear, but it was glorious. Her lungs filled with air, expanding painfully at first, but then beautifully.

I'm breathing again. I'm alive.

Her heart pounded in her chest, and the connection between her body and soul strengthened with every beat. But there was one thing she longed for more than anything.

I need to see him.

The darkness receded, inch by inch, and Aurora knew that soon, her eyes would open. When they did, the first thing she wanted to see was his face.

"Hey!"

Her eyes filled with tears. It was all the confirmation he needed. "Hi," she whispered. She held out her arms and he went into them, pulling her off the bed. He stroked her hair as she sobbed quietly into his shoulder. "I love you, Malik. I was so afraid I'd lost my chance to tell you." Burying his face in her hair, he rocked her, soothed her, and murmured his love for her.

Helios had moved to the far corner of the room conversing with Aceso and Alvaden. Malik had been so stunned to see his old friend here, that Alvaden had laughed riotously at the look on his face and Malik hadn't been able to verbalize what it meant to him: that seeing him here and happy with the woman he loved had given him more hope than anything had in his entire existence. Even more, than that damn crazy God appearing as if by magic in his torture chamber.

But hope was short-lived, no one had said anything about freeing him; they'd only allowed him to come to the surface to help Aurora. He didn't have the heart to tell her right now that he couldn't stay with her. It never would've worked anyway, because of what he was. All he could hope for was to find some way to survive, and maybe one day, ages from now, he would see her in all her godly splendor.

Aurora drew away from him, holding his face with both hands. She kissed him, her sweetness a balm to his weary, pain-riddled body. What he wouldn't give to take her home, spend a few hours in her arms letting her put him back together again. Maybe Helios would allow him that much. It wasn't as if he had anywhere to run.

"There are too many people or whatever in this room," she said impishly against his lips. She had the same ideas as him. "Can we go home now?"

"Aurora…I wish it were that simple." Her blue eyes searched his. A single tear trembled on her bottom eyelashes. "What do you mean?"

"I was only brought here to help you. I can't…" The tears spilled. Her expression shattered. "What? No."

"Shh. You know it's for the best."

"But it isn't. It isn't the best for me. There has to be someone I can talk to or—"

"No, I'm afraid that isn't possible."

"Malik, you can't leave me. We have to try anything. Do you want to stay?" He could lie, tell her he didn't. It would break her heart, but maybe it would put any outlandish ideas out of her head. In the end, he couldn't say the words. There'd been too many lies between them, and he never wanted to speak anything other than the truth to her again. "More than anything, love. But I can't. There isn't anything to be done about it."

There was a sound at his back, and Malik turned to see Helios standing just behind him. "I'm afraid it's time to go." Malik nodded, disentangling himself from Aurora's arms. It felt like leaving a limb behind. "I'm ready."

"You can't take him away from me!" she burst out, her sudden devastated fury focused all on the God.

"Aurora, it's going to be all right—" Malik began, but Helios cut him off. "The order was only good for him to save your life, Aurora. Whatever punishment his masters see fit to dole out, it still stands. The Caliphate won't get involved in that."

"Why not? It sounds like they can do whatever they want!" she fired back. "Please, Helios—"

"It's not my decision to make."

"But you talked them into this much. Surely you can do something."

"What I can't do is disobey their orders, which state I'm to return him once you have been restored. It's been done." Her voice cracked on her next words. "No, it hasn't. I'm not restored." She dissolved into sobs. Quietly, Malik pulled her head to his chest and looked up at Helios. "Can you give us a few minutes alone?" His mouth thinned with uncertainty, but he finally gave a curt nod and walked away, warning them he would be just outside the door. Alvaden and Aceso followed, their expressions grim.

"Aurora," he murmured, trying to get through to her over her racking sobs. They were so severe she could hardly breathe around them. "Listen to me. You're going to get over this. You're going to leave here and get on with your life, and things will be a lot better for you than they ever have been. Forget about me and live your life." Somehow, words formed from the hiccups tearing from her throat, but he thought surely, he misunderstood them. "You should have done it."

"Done what?"

"You should have taken me when you had the chance. You wouldn't be in all this trouble, and I could be with you."

The statement sparked such a vile reaction in him, he had her face in his hands and her head tilted back before he realized it. She gave a tiny gasp as his gaze bored into hers, and he spoke with such emphasis that each word shook her. "Don't say that. Don't even think that. Everything that's happened here today, everything we've done, was to keep you safe."

"I don't care."

"Yes, you do. You're irrational."

"I don't care," she repeated, practically snarling at him. "Don't tell me I'm fucking irrational when for the first time in my life, I know exactly what I want and where I belong. That's with you, wherever I have to go. I want you. Take me." Her hands slithered up over his shoulder, fingers kneading. Aghast at her determination and the dark, violent passion it stirred in him, he fought the urge to leap off the bed and put as much distance between them as possible. She'd just handed him her soul on a platter, after everything he'd gone through to let it go.

"You don't know what you're saying," he hissed, but his hands didn't release her. Cold blackness welled inside him, a chilling void that would draw her into it if he didn't keep it in check. "You have no idea what you'll be giving up."

"I'll be giving you up if I stay and that's too much."

"Has Helios told you that you are like him but trapped within yourself? Aurora, think about it. Everything you've done, every life you've lived, all the good things you've done, all the pain and the trials, every bit of it has been leading up to that. To what you told me you wanted, to be a part of something bigger than yourself."

"Maybe it's all been leading up to you." His breath hitched, stuttered, and stopped. "It's out of the question." The words strangled him. With a sudden burst of effort, he shoved her hands away and stood, pacing from the bed to stare out the window.

Outside, it was a picturesque spring morning. Inside, he felt all of the winter collected in his heart. There was a rustle behind him, and he turned to see Aurora on her feet moving toward the door. "What are you doing? You should rest."

"I'm fine." He moved to get in front of her and guide her back to her bed, but she shoved at him with a strength that surprised him.

"Get out of my way."

"Where the fuck are you going?"

"I'm going to talk to Helios." Oh, hellfire, that would spell disaster. "That isn't…advisable at the moment."

"It's advisable for you to get out of my way, Malik. I've been a pawn in your game my entire life. Do you realize that? And now you stand there and make this decision for me? I won't have it."

He could only stand and watch as this little mortal woman defeated him. *Again.* She pushed past him, staggering on her unsteady feet but throwing off any of his attempts to help her. He could only follow her into the hallway and stand uselessly behind her as she caught the attention of the God who'd been talking to Aceso. Helios frowned as he saw her. "You should—"

"No, I shouldn't. I want you to know that if Malik has to go back to Hell, then I go too."

"Aurora!" both Aceso and Helios snapped as if they were shocked parents dealing with an unruly teenager. Helios gazed up over her shoulder, connccting with Malik's and glowing impossibly blue. "This is your idea of helping the situation? You son of a—"

"Hey, don't look at me. This is all her."

"Because you've poisoned her mind!"

"For the first time in my life, my mind is clear but is it true what he just told me?" she asked.

"He said I'm like you." Helios's glare sharpened if that were even possible.

"Ordinarily you're not told you have to remember on your—"

"See, that's my problem with this whole thing all this secrecy, all this planning and plotting I'm utterly unaware of. Is it that way with everyone? Is this all just a big game between you all, an eternal power struggle? Is that the meaning of life?" She scoffed. "Then I don't care about living anymore. I don't care about being one of you. I want to make my own decision, and I choose to be with him. I love him and he loves me because I know what he was willing to give up for me. You can't tell me there was anything poisonous about it."

"I was standing there when they said he was as good as dead if he came to help you. If you go and they kill him, Aurora, you'll be alone and in more misery than—"

"If I stay here, I'll be alone and in misery. If I go, maybe they'll spare him. This was all about me in the first place, wasn't it? It can only help if he delivers me like he was supposed to."

"The problem with your logic is you're forgetting who you're dealing with."

"No, I'm not. I'm standing right next to one of them."

"She's got a point there," Aceso said, not too happy about Helios's last statement. Malik had scarcely been able to breathe through this exchange. Helios had lost his animosity while watching Aurora's tirade, and he stared at her now with increasing heartbreak. After a long, silent moment, he looked back up at Malik. "She's declared her wishes. She's yours. It's up to you."

Chapter 18

Gently, Malik took her shoulders and turned her to face him. "Aurora, I can't take you away from the sunlight and this world you love, the people you love. Don't ask me to do it."

"Is it that bad?"

"Yes," three voices chorused at once.

"But I'm used to it," he added. "You're not."

Her lower lip quivered. "I won't get used to it in time?" He stared at her, considering. Who was to say? With him at her side, if he could stay at her side and not meet a grisly end she might glory in the darkness. He thought of that first night in her apartment, staring down at her, her face split by light from the window. Half in light, half in shadow each equally beautiful. Aurora had as much darkness in her as she had light. Maybe he'd been the one to put it there, but it was a part of her now and she would carry it with her always.

"I want you to think about it," he said. "I don't want you to make any hasty decisions you'll regret."

"And you'll regret this one," Helios grumbled.

"Hey," Aceso said, giving Helios's arm a shove. "You've said your piece. Thank you. But you haven't thought to ask the opinion of the one who did give up everything for one of them."

"Look," Aceso said, taking Aurora's hands. "When they stripped my wings and cast me to earth for loving a demon, they might as well have sent me to Hell for the shock of it. I came to earth often before that, but fitting into life here was another matter. For a long time, I was alone. I didn't have Alvaden, but he haunted my every moment, waking or sleeping. When I finally saw him again—it made it all worth it. Do I wish things could be different? Yes, of course, but would I do it all again?" She smiled. "In a heartbeat. For him."

"Thank you," Aurora said quietly, a calm settling over her features as if this was the confirmation she'd been waiting for. "I want you to think about it too," Aceso said. "I didn't have a choice, but you do. I can't say what you'll face if you go there." She eyed Malik warily. "I'd be very careful if I were you."

"You don't even have to tell me." He was considering this, then. If he were honest with himself, he'd know he was considering it from the moment she suggested it. Rubbing a hand over Aurora's shoulder, he said, "It's you I'm worried about. If you end up there alone…"

"Malik, you were willing to sacrifice yourself for me. How would I be worthy of that if I'm not willing to do the same for you?" She wanted to be worthy of him. What backward alternate universe had Helios dropped him into? He couldn't speak; he could only look at her blue eyes and soft, trembling mouth. Look at her and know he could never be without her as long as he was alive.

Malik stood, holding Aurora's gaze, the weight of what she was offering settling in his chest. Her determination and willingness to follow him into Hell, to leave behind everything she knew, shook him to his core.

He took a deep breath and without breaking eye contact with Aurora spoke up. "I have an idea," he said softly, though his words were aimed at Helios than anyone else.

The God, standing near the door with his arms crossed and his back mostly turned, slowly pivoted to face Malik. "What is it now?" he asked, his voice tinged with exasperation.

Malik's grip on Aurora tightened for a moment before he let her go and stepped forward to face the god directly. "I need your help," he said, keeping his tone calm but firm. "There has to be another way—another way to free me without dragging her into Hell."

Helios raised an eyebrow. "You've already asked for more than any demon deserves. You were granted a chance to save her, and now you want more?"

Malik didn't flinch. "She wants more. She wants a future with me and I want to give her that without condemning her to eternal darkness."

Helios stared at him, then shifted his gaze to Aurora, who stood tall behind him, her chin raised in defiance. The God seemed to contemplate something, a frown deepening on his usually serene features.

Finally, Helios spoke. "Do you know what you're asking, Malakiás? What you're asking of The Caliphate?"

"I'm not asking for her to come to Hell with me," he clarified, his voice quieter. "I'm asking for a way out for both of us. She's been a part of your plans and your greater designs all along. You can't expect her to be happy if you send me back."

"It's unprecedented," Helios muttered, his gaze flickering with something like hesitation.

"Maybe," he agreed. "But you know as well as I do that if I return without her, the punishment will be worse than death. I've already defied my master there's no going back now."

Helios's eyes narrowed as he considered the demon's words. "And what makes you think I should care what happens to you?"

Malik's jaw tightened. "Because if I die, and she's left alone, then you've wasted centuries of watching her. She'll never reach her full potential as a goddess. You'll have failed."

Aurora stepped forward, her hand sliding into Malik's as she faced Helios. Her voice, though shaky, held a strength that resonated through the room. "I want to be with him," she said softly but with conviction. "But I also want to live. I want a future. And if that's with him, then I need to know it's possible."

The room fell silent for a moment, the weight of her words lingering. Aceso watched from the side, her arms crossed but her face showing a hint of sympathy.

Finally, Helios sighed. "You're asking for something that hasn't been done in millennia. The gods rarely offer mercy to those who cross their boundaries, and you've crossed them all."

"I'm not asking for mercy," Malik said, his voice low but steady. "I'm asking for a choice."

The god regarded them both for a long moment, his expression unreadable. Then, with a deep breath, Helios spoke. "I'll petition The Caliphate for one final chance," he said, his tone laced with warning. "But know this if they agree, it will not be easy. There will be conditions, and you may not like them."

Malik nodded, his heart pounding in his chest. "I'll take whatever they give."

Helios's gaze shifted to Aurora. "And you? Are you truly prepared to face whatever may come? There are no guarantees here."

Her grip on Malik's hand tightened. She looked into his eyes, her resolve unshaken. "I am. I'll face whatever it takes to stay with him."

Helios sighed, shaking his head as if he couldn't believe what he was about to do. "Very well," he said at last. "I'll speak to The Caliphate. But understand this—it's out of my hands now. Whatever they decide, you'll have to live with it."

Malik swallowed hard, feeling both relief and dread wash over him. "Thank you."

Helios turned and moved toward the door. "You'd better hope they find this proposal…interesting enough to entertain."

As he left the room, silence settled over them. Malik looked down at Aurora staring up at him with tear-filled eyes. He cupped her face gently, brushing away the tears with his thumb.

"We'll find a way," he whispered.

She nodded, though her expression remained uncertain. "I believe you."

As they stood there, wrapped in each other's presence, the weight of the unknown loomed large. They had no idea what The Caliphate would decide or what trials they might have to face. But for now, they had each other and that was enough.

Chapter 19

She wanted to tell him she found this all pretty messed up. But the words never left her lips. Helios didn't owe them anything tonight he could've just escorted Malik back to Hell like he was supposed to. Despite his stance on demons, he'd agreed to give their insane plan a chance.

"You wouldn't happen to be a hopeless romantic, would you?" she teased, trying to lighten the mood.

Helios chuckled softly. "Not at all. I leave that to the fickle mortal heart."

"Oh, so I'm fickle now?"

"No, not you. Obviously not."

She reached out, her fingers brushing against his hand resting on the rail. She half-expected them to pass right through, but his hand was as solid as hers, though cooler to the touch. "Thank you. You've done so much for me, and you didn't have to. I'm sorry I yelled at you earlier. And I'm sorry I can't be everything you want me to be. It's not that I don't want to…"

"Aurora," he interrupted, turning to face her. His hands rested gently on her shoulders, steadying her. "You already are. You're headstrong, loving, self-sacrificing, and innately good. You won't lose that, even if you never wear golden robes. It's okay."

Her throat tightened, tears pricking her eyes. She nodded, swallowing hard. "Thank you. Can I… can I hug you?"

"You'd better."

She hesitated unsure of where to put her arms around him with his wings in the way. But she managed, awkwardly at first, and then felt the warmth of his embrace. Maybe, just maybe, some of his light would rub off on her, because she needed it now more than ever.

Inside the bedroom, Malik waited, giving them their space. His expression was unreadable, a shadow over the room's soft, pastel décor. As Helios left, he and Malik exchanged curt nods, the tension between them thick but unspoken.

God, she did love him.

The weight hit her like a tidal wave as Malik opened his arms. Without hesitation, she rushed into them, burying herself in his embrace. The tears she'd held back with Helios now spilled freely, her body trembling as she clung to him, the only anchor she had left in the storm swirling around them.

"Make love to me," she whispered, her voice barely audible. "I need to be with you, one last time… like this." The words had scarcely left her lips when his mouth found hers, soft but urgent. Their clothes were soon discarded piece by piece in a slow, deliberate reveal. She knew they both savored every second of it.

When her gaze fell on the bruises and marks scattered across his body, her breath hitched, and she bit back a curse. Fresh tears welled in her eyes, though she thought she had none to shed.

"They hurt you," she murmured, her fingertips barely grazing the angry red welts along his skin.

"Already healing," he reassured her, brushing a brief, tender kiss against her lips. "I'm resilient. All I could think about was getting back to you."

"Oh, Malik, I love you." The words felt inadequate, too small for the depth of what she wanted to express. She longed to give him all the love he'd never known, all the tenderness he deserved. Instead of trying to speak it, she let her kiss say everything, her touch gentle against his bruised flesh. There were so many wounds that it felt impossible to avoid them, yet he never flinched, never pulled away. If anything, his desire only grew stronger.

He kissed her deeply, his hands tracing her body with a devotion that left her trembling. He explored every inch of her, her breasts, her thighs, her belly lingering in a slow, teasing rhythm that left her aching. He deliberately avoided the place where she needed him most, and the frustration built until she was on the edge of begging. Finally, when his fingers found her, slick and ready, her breath hitched.

He waited, hovering just at the brink, until the tip of his cock pressed against her entrance. In that suspended moment, he returned her words.

"I love you, Aurora," he whispered, then sank into her, his kiss muffling her cry. His movements were slow and deliberate, each stroke pushing her closer to the edge, sending her spiraling into bliss. Again and again, he brought her to the heights of pleasure, each wave more intoxicating than the last. With nothing between them, the connection was raw, electric. When he finally came, she felt all the warmth, the shudder that ran through his body, his groan heavy against her ear. At that moment she realized a wholeness she hadn't known was missing.

As they lay together afterward, breathless and spent, he touched her cheek, his eyes softened with something deeper than lust.

"I had it all wrong," he said quietly.

"Hmm?" She glanced at him, her eyelids heavy with exhaustion and contentment.

"I was wrong," he continued, his thumb brushing her skin. "I always thought you belonged to me, but it was the other way around. I belong to you if I had a soul, you stole it centuries ago."

She smiled dreamily at him, letting herself get lost in his eyes. Whatever they would face tonight, they'd face it together. It was going to work. It had to. "No matter what I said the other day in my apartment, I'm yours. This is one soul you didn't have to steal."

***

"Well, here we are," Aurora said with a small, nervous laugh. A few hours passed since they had first laid out the plan. She and Malik now sat facing each other on the bed, while Helios stood silently nearby. As much as she would have loved to stay wrapped up in his arms it was time to see if their desperate, crazy plan would work.

Malik nodded, his expression unreadable. "After everything we've been through, I never thought it would come to this."

She reached up, cupping his face with her hand. His lips instinctively brushed against her palm. "It's going to be all right," she said softly. "Don't you think so?"

His golden eyes, usually so darkened, seemed to glimmer for a brief moment. "If I didn't think there was a chance, I wouldn't be here."

"Okay." Somehow, his faint flicker of hope was enough to steady her. "I'm ready."

More than anything, she feared the unbearable pain she'd felt when the other demon had attacked her the memory of that searing, scalding heat still haunted her. He must have sensed her fear because he took her hand, locking his gaze with hers.

"It'll only hurt until you're detached," he said softly. "Once you're completely free, the pain will stop."

Panic fluttered inside her chest, memories of the black void rushing back. "Will I be able to, see? Hear?"

"Yes," he promised. "But not in the way you do now. You'll sense everything. You'll know I'm with you."

She nodded, taking a deep breath to steady herself. "Okay."

Helios stepped forward, extending his hand. "Take mine," he said. She obeyed, gripping Malik's hand with her other. The sensation of holding both of them one warm, the other cool sent an odd, electric jolt through her body.

"Please, make it fast," she whispered, her voice betraying her sudden vulnerability.

Malik's eyes never left hers. His unreadable gaze seemed to expand, filling her entire world. Power stirred behind his eyes, visible and potent. She almost wanted to pull away, to escape what was coming but he didn't give her the chance. His hand shot to her chest, and a sudden, unbearable agony ripped through her. She had just enough time to let out a cry before his fingers twisted and pulled, and it was over.

The world dimmed, blurring into an incomprehensible haze. Voices echoed distantly Malik's reassuring words: "I've got you. It's all right." Helios urged him to hurry, telling him they didn't have much time, there was no time to adjust to the strange new sensation before she fell, wind rushing all around her.

She clung to Malik, his arms locked tightly around her, anchoring her as they hurtled through the abyss. The fall seemed endless as if they would plummet forever. But then, just as abruptly, it stopped.

Everything stopped.

"Aurora, look," he said, his voice soft near her ear did she even have ears? Could she still, see?

Her face had been buried against his chest, and when he pulled back, she realized the darkness wasn't a void but the shadow of his body. She felt solid again, real.

She lifted her head and saw where they had landed.

They stood on a jagged outcropping before a massive, looming structure—a castle, unlike any castle she had ever seen. It defied logic, with staircases spiraling into nothingness and doorways leading nowhere. Overhead, black clouds churned, flickering with red and orange lightning. Below them, the ground was nothing but fire. The landscape stretched out, a hellish expanse of charred rock, lava, and seething flames. And the souls of those tormented, dead-eyed figures she had seen in her nightmares were everywhere, crawling in agony, clawing to escape only to be dragged back by invisible forces.

It was every nightmare she'd ever had, brought to life.

"This is my home," he said, his voice tight. She looked up at him and saw that, for the first time, his eyes reflected the light around them, the flickering glow of the inferno mirrored in his gaze.

She tried to take a breath but found she couldn't. The air was thick and toxic, though it no longer mattered. Her lungs weren't working. Panic flared as she clawed at her throat, gasping for air she couldn't find.

He noticed her distress and grabbed her hands, pulling them away from her neck. "Aurora," he said gently, "you don't need to breathe. You have no lungs, no beating heart. You're only remembering the need for those things. Just let go. You won't suffocate."

She stared at him, the truth crashing down on her. She was dead. She had let him kill her. She had trusted him with everything. What if it had been a trick? What if she had made the biggest mistake of her life ... of her death?

No, she couldn't think that way. This was Malik. He'd shown her everything, even this horrible place because he trusted her. She couldn't turn back now.

"Who are they?" she asked, her voice shaking as she watched the writhing souls in the flames.

"The damned," he said. "The worst of the worst."

"They're the ones I saw before… the ones who haunted me."

He nodded. "I thought as much."

Despite the terror gripping her, she forced herself to stand tall. She refused to cling to him, even though every part of her wanted to hide in his arms. She lifted her chin and looked into his eyes. "Malik, it's awful here, but I'm not afraid. I won't run."

A muscle in his jaw clenched. "You haven't seen everything yet."

She would have swallowed if she could. As she watched, something dark began to swirl around him, smoky tendrils encircling his body. Slowly, the darkness consumed him, transforming him into something far larger, more menacing. When the smoke finally cleared, she forced herself to keep looking.

What stood before her was a demon. Shadowed dark scales covered his body, black wings spread wide behind him and terrible claws replaced his hands. She barely recognized him.

"Aurora," his voice growled, deeper now but still unmistakably him. "Look at me. This is what you're choosing. Look at what you're willing to spend eternity with."

She could feel the tears welling up again, burning as they dripped onto the scorched ground beneath her feet. But she looked at him. She owed him that much. Beneath the monstrous exterior, she could still see him the man she loved. His brow was ridged, horns curled like a ram's, but his eyes were the same. His wings, though, were torn and scarred. They had tortured him, humiliated him, and he had let them... for her.

"Just let me go," he pleaded. "Let me take you back and live your life forget about me."

Without hesitation, she stepped toward him, her hands resting on his chest, her lips brushing a kiss over one of his wounds. His name rumbled from his chest, a broken growl, as he placed his hand on her head with surprising gentleness.

"I'm not running," she whispered, looking up at him. "So, what else have you got?"

With a strangled sound, he dropped to his knees before her, gripping her arms. His face, twisted with heartbreak, broke her completely. "You can't stay here."

"I have to," she said softly, touching his face, her hands trembling. "I have to save you. It's not about me. I'm staying because I love you."

He clung to her, his arms tightening as if holding on for dear life. She leaned into him, whispering, "I love you," as her tears fell onto his head.

And beneath them, the ground trembled.

Chapter 20

The fact Aurora should this place or see him like this was insufferable. He could end it all right now. Just seize her and take her back to her waiting body, where Helios kept her animated for her return. He'd insisted on that much, but the clock was ticking maybe an hour, if that. Time was unpredictable here, slipping away like sand. If he didn't get her back soon it would be too late.

Malik knew all of this. Yet still, he hadn't acted.

What if it worked? What if she could stay and be his? If she was willing to face this, to give up everything for him what argument was there left to make?

Without a word, he led her toward the keep the only way this would work was if Ordog saw her, approved her, and declared Malik spared. But the thought chilled him. His heart, if it still functioned like one, felt like a block of ice rattling in his chest. He could imagine Helios showing up, using that amulet to knock some sense into him, and he would probably let him.

The inside of the keep was worse than the hellscape outside. He guided her forward, avoiding the horror in the chambers they passed, shielding her from as much as he could. Screams echoed in the distance, each one making her flinch, and every sound pulled him back to his own time spent hanging helpless in the dungeon. He'd die before they put him back in that place. Ordog better be ready for a fight.

At last, they reached the massive doors to Ordog's chamber. He turned to her, his grip on her arm tightening. "This is it. Are you ready?"

"No," she whispered, "but I don't have a choice."

Malik managed a small, strained smile. She was just a faded image of herself here, but still so beautiful it ached. He couldn't believe he'd once wanted this for her. He had so much to make up for and was ready to start.

"Let me do the talking. No matter what I say, go along with it. Show no fear. They feed on it." She nodded, trying to hide her fear. "Good. Let's go."

He shoved open the heavy doors. Ordog sat on his ridiculous throne, surrounded by others. Kimaris was among them, the smug bastard. Aurora faltered at the sight of him, but he forced her forward, ignoring the tiny sob that escaped her. They couldn't afford weakness now.

The chamber was vast and dark, illuminated only by flickering torches. All eyes turned toward them, a mix of humanoid and beastly gazes. She hesitated, but he pushed her ahead, desperate to keep her from freezing under their scrutiny. He needed her to hold it together, or they wouldn't make it out of here.

Ordog raised a brow, finger tapping pensively at his lips. "Well, well," he drawled.

"You wanted me to bring her," he said, pulling her to the front of the throne. "Here she is."

"I see you've come to your senses." Ordog rose slowly from his chair, descending the dais with a deliberate, predatory air. Aurora recoiled, pressing back against Malik, but he held her firm. Ordog's red eyes gleamed as they roved over her, hungry and lecherous. Malik's blood boiled.

When Ordog reached out to touch her cheek, Malik yanked her back, wrapping his arm protectively around her. "No," he snarled.

Ordog's eyes narrowed. "One request?" he asked, his voice dangerously low.

"It's the only one I make," he replied coldly. "Let her be mine, and only mine to do with as I wish."

Kimaris chuckled. "Where's the fun in that?"

Ordog's hand fell to his side. "How selfish of you it would be such a shame if she couldn't… enjoy all of our attention."

Malik's arm tightened around her as she trembled against him. "I can return her if my conditions aren't met," he said, his voice even, but sharp. "Gods are waiting to place her under divine protection if I do any demon who touches her would be signing their death warrant."

The room fell into a stunned silence. Even Ordog paused mid-step, his black cape swirling. He spun on his heel, eyes blazing. "What do you mean, return her?"

"Exactly what I said." his voice remained calm, though the tension in the air was suffocating. "Truthfully, I brought her here fully intending to take her back." Aurora looked at him in shock, but he kept his eyes on Ordog.

"And why is she here now?" he demanded, his red eyes narrowing.

"I'm here because I want to be," she answered quietly.

Malik's heart sank. He tightened his grip on her in warning, but she was undeterred.

"I'm here because I love him."

The room recoiled and the ground trembled beneath their feet, just as it had the first time she'd said those words.

Ordog's face twisted in rage. "What have you done? You fool."

"You shall cleanse the abomination, cast out the afflicted, for it is an offense too vile for even Hell to endure."

The words from Ordog's study crashed into Malik's mind of course.... *Love.* An abomination that Hell itself couldn't bear. He'd brought love into the one place it could not exist.

Ordog's hands trembled with fury. "You threaten the very foundations of this realm! Is that what you want, Malakiás?"

"I only want her, however, I can have her."

"Haven't you learned?" Ordog snarled. "Hell cannot suffer a soul capable of love. I should kill you where you stand."

Malik let out a bitter laugh. "You're always saying that. Isn't it time you actually tried?"

A glowing pike of flame materialized in Ordog's hand, casting an orange glow through the chamber. Malik nudged Auora back, drawing his own weapon a heavy, fiery scythe.

"So, we've let it come to this," Malik muttered as they circled each other.

"You've let it come to this," Ordog spat. "I should make you suffer, but I'm tired of your games."

Then he lunged their weapons, clashed, and sparks flying as they traded blow after blow. They were too well-matched, each anticipating the other's moves. Aurora gasped from the side, a sound that tore at Malik's focus. He couldn't afford to lose control now, but every time he heard her, his heart lurched.

Ordog aimed for his chest, but Malik parried, sweeping low and knocking him off his feet. Ordog rolled, narrowly avoiding Malik's scythe as it crashed into the floor. Before Malik could recover, Ordog kicked him hard in the knee, sending him crashing down.

They grappled on the ground, tearing at each other with claws and teeth. Malik was stronger, but Ordog had the advantage. Until...

Aurora screamed one of the other demons had his filthy claws on her. Something inside Malik snapped. With a roar, he shoved Ordog off him, slamming into the demon that had grabbed her. They hit the ground hard, Malik's rage giving him the strength to tear him away from her.

The ground shook beneath them, stronger than before. Malik knew Ordog was right, he couldn't defeat them all.

He wouldn't last much longer but maybe, he could use the one weapon left to him: his voice.

Panting, Malik scrambled to his feet. "Did you feel that?" he asked, his voice loud enough for all to hear. "Every time she says she loves me, she threatens this place. What if I let her say it over and over until this keep is nothing but rubble?"

"You think—"

"I *know*," he smirked through his bloodied lips. "The rule is clear. Hell cannot hold a soul that loves. You know it, Ordog."

Ordog froze, staring at Malik, his fiery pike flickering out. Silence fell over the chamber.

"You… are not worthy of death," he finally said, his voice filled with disgust. "Get out of my sight. You are banished from the kingdom of the Dark Lord. Go live with your human and see how long her world tolerates you."

Malik didn't dare move. From her place on the floor, Aurora looked up at him, wide-eyed. They had done it.

"Go!" Ordog roared. "Before she destroys us all!"

Malik didn't wait for another word. He grabbed her hand and pulled her up, leading her out of the chamber. A grin tugged at his lips. Whether she wanted to be or not his little goddess just saved them.

It felt so good—*too* good—to be normal again. Aurora had meant it when she said she would stay in Hell with him but damn, she was glad she didn't have to. Waking up here felt like breaking free from a nightmare, her relief so intensely it was almost painful.

Helios looked like a kid on Christmas morning as her eyes fluttered open, and Malik hung his head in visible relief.

"Well?" Helios asked eagerly.

"I nearly destroyed Hell," she said with a smirk.

Malik chuckled, and Helios rolled his eyes heavenward. "If only we could be so lucky."

"I was banished," Malik added. "All in all, a productive trip."

"Banished? Interesting." Helios tilted his head. "Hell doesn't want you, and Heaven won't have you. What will you do?"

Malik glanced down at Aurora, and she saw the exhaustion in his eyes. She thought about ways she'd like to add to that weariness in much more pleasurable ways but for now, she smiled and squeezed his hand.

"Be loved," he finished softly.

"That much is certain," she said.

"You know," Helios said, looking thoughtful, "Aceso can help you get what you need to live among mortals. If you're no longer Hell's minion there's no harm in us assisting, you."

"Really?" Aurora perked up, trying to sit up. Both Malik and Helios helped her, and though she was still weak, she felt better than the last time Malik had revived her.

"We'll need to figure this out," she said, glancing at Malik. "You're banished, but you're not human. You're still immortal, right?"

"It seems so," he said. "I still had the power to bring you back, so nothing's been stripped away."

She sighed, a thought crossing her mind. "Am I going to have to get old and gray while you still look like… this?" She waved a hand at him. "Not that I'm complaining," she quickly added, seeing his incredulous expression. "But it might cause some uh, problems, you know?"

Malik grinned. "I can appear any age I want. I just prefer this one." He winked. "But if you want me to look like a wrinkled old man someday, I can do that. For you."

"Thanks… I think." She giggled, but then a shadow passed over her thoughts. "But what about… after I'm gone?"

"Let's not dwell on that just yet," Helios said, his voice firm with optimism. "Go, live a long and happy life together it's more than most people get. We'll deal with that when the time comes. I'll still be around, of course." He winked at her, a surprisingly mischievous gesture that made her raise an eyebrow.

A long and happy life. The sound of it warmed her, wrapping her in a quiet joy. It was much better than the dark and miserable eternity she had once feared.

Epilogue

"Are you sure you want to do this?" Malik asked quietly.

"No," she admitted, her breath clouding in the cold air. "But it's something I need to do. Thanks for coming with me." She knocked on the door for the third time, her fist hesitant but determined. Maybe he wasn't home, he didn't open the door to strangers, maybe they'd come all this way for nothing.

Malik glanced down the quiet street behind them, muttering, "He's not going to be happy to see me, he'll probably have a heart attack."

Aurora almost smiled, maybe her father didn't open the door for demons who had tempted him into trading his daughter's soul nearly thirty years ago. That could be it. "Well, for that matter, he might not be happy to see me either."

"I can sit in the car if you think it'll help."

"No," she said quickly, reaching for his gloved hand. His warmth was a comfort in the biting cold. Snow dusted the carefully tended lawns, Christmas lights twinkling from houses up and down the street. The yard had a Santa waving from his sleigh, while his small house was draped in colorful, blinking lights. "I want you here."

He smiled softly, and she took a moment to appreciate how beautiful he looked, ice crystals catching in his dark hair. The last couple of years with him had been the happiest of her life, and she didn't think that happiness would fade anytime soon.

This was crazy, no doubt. But if what Malik said was true and he had turned his life around after making the deal he must carry tremendous guilt. He had told her what kind of man he'd been before a man trapped in drugs, crime, and desperation. But her father had changed, helped his community, and counseled troubled youth. Even Helios had confirmed that even Heaven had been watching him, but he was sick now, and there wasn't much time left.

Yes, it was a terrible thing he'd done but she wanted to give him peace. She wanted him to know she was okay and that his mistake had brought something unexpectedly good into her life.

She pounded harder on the door, urgency pushing her. She had to know. She didn't fully understand why it was so important, but it gnawed at her, keeping her awake at night, whispering in the back of her mind.

Suddenly, the door swung open mid-knock, and Aurora froze, arm raised awkwardly. Malik turned toward the doorway, his gaze sharp.

An older woman with graying hair stood framed in the doorway, eyeing them curiously. "Yes?"

"Um, hello," Aurora stammered. "Does Andreas Rayner live here?"

"He does." The woman's eyes narrowed slightly. "And you are?"

"My name is Aurora DeBorealis. He may not know me, but…" She took a steadying breath. "I'm his daughter."

The woman's eyebrows shot up, and she pulled her blue cardigan tighter against the cold. "You're Aurora?"

"You… know my name?"

"Honey, he's been talking about a daughter named Aurora for as long as I've known him, but he never knew your last name, or how to find you. I always wondered if you really existed."

"And you are…?"

"I'm his wife, Beth." She extended a hand, still looking stunned. Aurora shook it, feeling equally disoriented. This felt surreal. "I'm afraid he's not doing well right now."

"I'd heard he was ill. I'm so sorry."

Beth nodded, wiping at her eyes before slipping her glasses back on. "It's just… a lot to take in you know?"

"I know," Aurora said softly, touching Beth's arm.

"Cancer," Beth explained with a shaky voice. "The treatments aren't working as well as they used to, and he's resting now. But he'd never forgive me if I didn't tell him, you were here."

"I don't want to disturb him—"

"Nonsense. Come in out of the cold before you freeze." She ushered them inside. "And who's this handsome man with you? Your husband?"

Just my demon lover.

"Oh, something like that," Malik said with a charming smile, earning a playful nudge from Aurora. "Call me Malik."

As they stepped into the warm house, the scent of coffee drifted from the kitchen. The living room was cozy, the walls filled with family photos, memories crowding every surface. At least it looked like her father had lived a happy life.

"I always suspected there was more to the story," Beth said, glancing nervously at Aurora. "He never really explained how he knew about you. He would mention your name, but nothing more. I've had a thousand questions over the years that he never answered."

"I'll do my best to answer them," Aurora said casting a glance at Malik.

"Please, make yourselves comfortable. I'll let him know you're here." Beth gestured to the couch and disappeared down the hallway.

Aurora sat down, her mind racing. "I think you should stay out here," she whispered to Malik. "Just in case I get to go back and see him."

He nodded, pulling her close. "That's probably best."

She sighed into his embrace, the warmth of his body grounding her in this strange, surreal moment. "If it weren't for you, he wouldn't even know my name, would he?"

He ran a hand through her hair. "I guess not, I'm the one who told him about you."

"My mom knew who he was, but she never reached out to him. No one did."

He kissed her forehead just as Beth reappeared at the doorway.

"Aurora?" Beth smiled. "He's awake. He's very excited to meet you."

She stood, reluctant to leave the comfort of Malik's arms. She held his hand as long as she could before finally letting go. He smiled at her, a glimmer of something unspoken in his eyes.

"Thank you," she mouthed to him before following Beth down the hall.

Bonus Material

In a world where the supernatural walks among mortals, fate weaves a treacherous path for those destined to unlock the mysteries of ancient powers and forbidden love. In **Crimson Allure**, three heroines are bound by their untapped potential and the dark, immortal forces that claim them, battling curses, ancient prophecies, and the seductive lure of the unknown.

In

Crimson Allure, each heroine's journey leads to an undeniable connection with the supernatural, where love is both their greatest strength and their darkest temptation.

Other Titles by Author

Seven of Sins

Recapturing Fate

Fires Within Series:

Book One: Fires Within

Fractured Desires Trilogy:

Book One: Cosa Nostra
Book Two: Apex

About the Author

Jezza Deep is an accomplished indie writer, poet, and anime critic with a distinct flair for storytelling that seamlessly blends mysticism, romance, mythology, and fairy tales. Her poetry has received international acclaim, with two of her works featured in the prestigious *International Library of Poetry* in 2003 and 2005.

She extends her creative talents through fiction, fractured fairy tales, fan fiction, and poetry, contributing to various platforms. As she continues to craft imaginative and thought-provoking works, Jezza Deep captivates readers with stories that transcend boundaries and resonate deeply.

Stay Connected with Jezza Deep

Website: https://bit.ly/JezzaDeep

LinkTree: https://bit.ly/4degxcb